"You look much better now."

"Oh, do I?" He laughed, his gray eyes almost black with bitter rage.

"Y-yes, you do look much better...."

"Handsome, am I?" He caught hold of her arms, his fingers biting into her flesh, and Luisa's nerves leapt in panic.

"Mr. West, please..."

"No need to beg—I'm going to give you what you want!"

She threw a look upward, her blue eyes wide with shock and alarm, and he laughed in angry mockery.

"Obviously you can't wait...."

Zachary West's mouth came down hard against hers and the world went out of focus for an endless moment....

CHARLOTTE LAMB is one of Harlequin's best-loved and bestselling authors. Her extraordinary career, in which she has written more than one hundred books, has helped shape the face of romance fiction around the world.

Born in the East End of London, Charlotte spent her early childhood moving from relative to relative to escape the bombings of World War II. After working as a secretary in the BBC's European department, she married a political reporter who wrote for *The Times.* Charlotte recalls that it was at his suggestion that she began to write, "because it was one job I could do without having to leave our five children." Charlotte and her family now live in a beautiful home on the Isle of Man. It is the perfect setting for an author who creates characters and stories that delight romance readers everywhere.

Books by Charlotte Lamb

HARLEQUIN PRESENTS PLUS

HARLEQUIN PRESENTS: BARBARY WHARF

CHARLOTTE LAMB
Dreaming

Harlequin Books

TORONTO • NEW YORK • LONDON
AMSTERDAM • PARIS • SYDNEY • HAMBURG
STOCKHOLM • ATHENS • TOKYO • MILAN
MADRID • WARSAW • BUDAPEST • AUCKLAND

ISBN 0-373-11618-7

DREAMING

CHAPTER ONE

ZACHARY WEST loaded the last canvas into the back of the van, then checked yet again that everything was securely fastened down. He didn't want any accidents *en route*. That was why he was taking the canvases himself, instead of sending them with the courier service Leo had wanted him to use.

'Much safer, Zac!' Leo had urged on the phone. 'And much less trouble for you! They'll pack them up; you won't have to do a thing!'

'I prefer to do it myself.'

'That's crazy, Zac. These people are experts! They——'

'I once lost a canvas when someone who was carrying it dropped it, fell over, and put a foot through it. Never again. I pack them up myself, and I'm driving them to London, too.'

'Why are you so stubborn, you irritating man?' Leo had demanded, but Zachary would not change his mind.

He thought long and hard before he did anything, but once he had made up his mind he didn't change it, whatever anybody said. In the last resort, he believed, you could only rely on yourself, and life had proved him right. Zachary West was grimly self-sufficient, and it showed.

His black leather jacket and jeans coupled with his height gave an almost menacing look to his rough black hair, razor-cut features and hard jawline. Of this Zachary was quite unaware, even when he got sideways looks of uneasiness from people in the street. He was rarely conscious of other people. His mind obsessed with his work, he had no time to waste on anything else.

He rarely went to London and there had been no woman in his life for a year or so, since he'd found out that his last girlfriend was dating someone else at the same time. Zachary had brutally told her what he thought of her and hadn't seen her since. He had barely thought of her, either, except when he found something of hers around the cottage— a handkerchief, still sweet with her perfume, a small comb, a red lipstick.

Frowning, he would get rid of them, but for a while the cottage would hold her presence: Dana's bright, seductive eyes and amused mouth hovering on the air like the smile of the Cheshire cat. Zachary exorcised it with relentless work.

When he wasn't painting he looked after the garden, grew his own vegetables and fruit, kept chickens so that he had free-range eggs whenever he needed them, and when the hens stopped laying eggs Zachary killed and cooked them to supplement his diet. He lived simply and did his own housework and washing.

The red-brick cottage had been built in the reign of Queen Anne for a retired sea captain who wanted to pretend he was still at sea. The house looked out over the windy coastline of Suffolk and in a gale the old timbers creaked and groaned as if they were at sea. Nothing had changed in that view in the last three hundred years; it was still a wild and lonely place with the savagery of the sea in front of it and behind it flat, low-lying fields with winding roads buried secretly among them.

The village, Tareton, was a mile away, the nearest little town, Whinbury, a good twenty-minute drive past that. That isolation was what had drawn Zachary to the place. Here he could work uninterrupted and without distractions and when he needed anything he couldn't get in the village shop—paints or canvases, for instance—he could always drive into Whinbury and there pick up the main road to London as he would be doing this evening.

The light was going as Zachary came out of the cottage again, locking the door behind him as he looked up at the darkening spring sky. It was early for twilight—was there rain in those clouds? He didn't enjoy driving long distances in the rain, especially at night. Grey eyes frowning, he looked at his watch. He should be in London by seven. With luck, the rain might hold off until then.

As he drove, he thought of the coming exhibition and all the turmoil which would accompany it. His mouth twisted cynically. Leo loved it, of course; he revelled in the Press showing, the society parties, the art critics with their reviews and their rich, smart friends. Zachary hated it.

He was dreading the whole experience; he should never have let Leo talk him into it. It wasn't his first exhibition, it was his third, but he had not had one for some years because he disliked them so much, and he didn't need to drum up custom. He wasn't a portrait painter, looking out for rich people to paint. He painted landscapes, still life; they sold well because people knew what they were about, they did not need to have them explained. Leo thought that...

At that instant, out of the corner of his eye, Zachary caught a flicker of white and instinctively turned his head. There it was again, a whiteness, floating sideways, above a leafy hedge, through the growing dusk.

'What on earth is that?'

He narrowed his eyes, but still couldn't make it out clearly. A piece of paper blowing in the wind? A white bird? A barn owl? One didn't often see their white faces haunting these lanes any more, but Zachary loved them and regretted that.

His foot hit the brake. As his van slowed he went on staring, the hair standing up on the back of his neck as the whiteness flowed on alongside him, on the other side of that hedge. No, that wasn't a bird, or an owl. What in the name of heaven was it?

Zachary didn't believe in ghosts, and disliked things he could not rationally explain. He was an artist, with trained eyes; he knew what tricks the eye could play, how the eye and brain together could deceive. There had to be an explanation, but what was it?

His van slowed almost to a stop as he reached a gate through which he saw a garden and behind that, at a great distance, along a tree-lined drive, the pale, shadowy shape of a large white house. The floating whiteness reached it too, a second later, and turned in the air.

As it did so, Zachary suddenly realised what he had seen, and began to laugh a little angrily because he felt a fool. Just for a second he had almost thought he saw a ghost.

But it was only a girl: a small, slender girl with long, straight dark hair, framing a pale oval face. Her head must have been turned away from the road, her dark hair hiding her face, making her head invisible to him.

That was why he hadn't realised he was watching a human being as she walked behind the hedge. All he had seen was the white dress she wore—a flowing garment with long, billowing sleeves. Now she leaned over a gate in the hedge, staring out into the road, clearly visible to him. Briefly, she looked across at Zachary, in his van, then her dark blue eyes moved on indifferently, to watch the road ahead of him, the road into Whinbury.

Grimacing, Zachary drove on. If he hadn't been in a hurry he would have stopped to ask her if she was human. Or was she a witch-girl weaving spells in the twilight? He laughed at himself again. Oh, come on! he told himself—stop thinking nonsense. At this time of the evening it was easy to let the imagination run riot, especially in a state of heightened excitement.

She was neither a ghost nor a witch-girl. But she had a strange, unearthly beauty; he couldn't help being curious about her and wondering what she had been doing, walking alone in the twilight garden. Who had she been waiting for? A lover? There had been a sense of urgency in her fixed waiting, the intentness of those blue eyes—and yet at the same time Zachary's antennae, the intuitions of an artist accustomed to reading what lay behind people's faces, had picked up no passion, no sensuality. There had been something else entirely in that face. What? he thought, frowning, trying to pin down his shifting impressions. Something almost nun-like: a purity in the oval of her face, in her widely spaced blue eyes, in her gentle pink mouth, as if she came from another plane, a spirit world.

Zachary remembered Dana, grimacing. There was a world of difference between the two girls! Now, Dana...

The road turned sharply on a bend at that point, and as Zachary began to take the corner a dark red car hurtled towards him from the other direction, but much too far over on Zachary's side of the road. Zachary swore, stiffening and turning pale. He slammed on his brake, swinging his wheel sharply to one side, but there was no chance of avoiding the red car. He hit it with a crash that sent his van skidding and spinning right across the road through a hedge.

He was flung violently forward, into his steering-wheel, his chest slamming into the padded leather.

His seatbelt held, though. He was pulled sharply back again as the impact of the collision filled the world with the sound of splintering glass, rending metal, screaming. His head hit the side of the door and he slumped, dazed, half unconscious for a moment, then his nostrils twitched, inhaling a pungent scent.

'Oh, my God...' he groaned, pulling himself together as he recognised the smell of petrol.

White-faced, he struggled to undo his seatbelt and get out of the van, but even as he felt the metal clasp give way, releasing him, there was a sudden whooshing sound and a wall of flame shot up in front of him. Fierce, searing heat blazed through the broken windscreen and Zachary gave a scream of agony as it hit him, his hands flung up in front of his face in a vain effort to shield himself from the flames.

The phone rang as Luisa was just starting out on her round, which had already been delayed endlessly by one crisis after another. She sighed as she picked up the phone. What else could go wrong? But her voice was soft and calm, betraying nothing of her thoughts. 'Burns Unit.'

'Sister Gilbey?' The voice was familiar and a faint smile touched her mouth and eyes, changing her whole expression.

'Yes, Mr Hallows,' she said demurely, because in the hospital they always tried to keep their outward relationship professional. David sounded tired, and no wonder. He had been in Theatre for hours.

'He's in Recovery and he'll be coming down to you in half an hour or so. I'm just sending you the papers. Considering the nature of the burns, he stood up to the operation pretty well. He's fit and tough; he should pull through. Shock's the immediate threat, of course. If he gets through the next twenty-four hours without a set-back the prognosis is hopeful.'

Luisa listened, frowning, her blue eyes dark with compassion. She had worked on this ward for several years now and was used to seeing men, women, and, even worse, children, with horrifying injuries, their faces and bodies badly burnt, but she never became hardened by custom; she was still moved and disturbed by what she saw.

'Lucky we aren't rushed off our feet at the moment. I'll be able to have one nurse monitoring him closely all night. Whatever nursing can do we'll do for him, poor man.'

'I know you will—you have a very good team down there,' David Hallows said warmly, then paused before adding, in a lower and more personal tone, 'Talking about not being rushed off your feet, does that mean you will be able to come to the dance on Saturday, after all?'

He had invited her several weeks ago and she had been hesitant, warning him that she might have to work this weekend because her senior staff nurse would be on holiday and she had another girl away with a broken leg. The ward roster had had to be rearranged, and Luisa wasn't sure whether or not she could get anyone to take charge of the ward on Saturday night.

'Well, I've had to compromise, David,' she said wryly. 'I've arranged with Staff Nurse Jenkins from Surgical to do a split shift. She was on this ward for a long time before she moved to Surgical, so she knows the routine. She'll work here from eight until two, and then I'll take over and finish the shift.'

'So you'll come to the dance with me?' His voice was pleased; she could imagine the smile on his calmly attractive face. David Hallows was not handsome, but he had a face people instinctively took to on sight. Warm brown eyes, set wide apart, direct and friendly; wide, placid cheekbones, a firm but kindly look to his mouth, and smooth brown hair—he was one of the most popular members of staff at Whinbury Hospital.

'I'd love to! Thank you for asking me, David.' Luisa had been out to dinner with him quite often over the past months, but they both knew that this invitation was different. At the hospital dance they would be very publicly paired off; everyone would be watching them, fascinated. In this closed community, people gossiped endlessly.

'A pity you can't have the whole night off! We could have gone on somewhere afterwards. Everyone else will be going back to Mack's place, I gather.'

She laughed. 'They usually do.'

'Ending up with bacon and eggs for breakfast at dawn!'

'Poor Mrs Mack—she's a long-suffering soul.'

'She seems to thrive on it, and being the wife of the chief consultant gives her a lot of status,' David said drily.

'I like her; she can be very kind.'

'Hmm . . . well, she throws her weight around too much for me—thinks she's Queen of Whinbury. I don't like bossy women.'

Luisa's eyes were amused; this confession was not news to her. She had seen David bristling whenever Mrs MacDonald appeared at the hospital. That regal manner didn't worry Luisa, who had spent her training being ordered around by autocratic senior nurses, but she knew it put David's back up.

He yawned then. 'Oh, well, I'm going to bed now, but I'm on call all night, if I'm needed.'

'You must be dead on your feet, poor David—I hope I won't have to wake you up. Sleep well.'

David hung up and Luisa replaced the phone and left her office. The ward was shadowy, curtains drawn around some of the beds, one of her nurses sitting constantly beside a patient who was still on the danger list. Some beds were empty, stripped down to the plastic cover and smelling strongly of the disinfectant with which they had been washed. In others, patients lay rigidly like Egyptian mummies, their bedclothes carefully raised over a cradle so that no weight should lie on their bodies. They were afraid to move: lay there, trapped in pain, only the sheen of their eyes as she walked past betraying that they were alive and awake, and suffering. Luisa walked from bed to bed on almost noiseless feet, at her customary measured pace, used to the half-dark of the ward, the pools of yellow light here and there. She whispered gently to those who were awake, soothed, promised pain-killers, paused to watch those who slept before walking on again.

She liked working at night. There was a very special feel to a ward during those long dark hours when the rest of the world slept, and only you were awake. You came much closer to the patients than you could during the day. Then they had their guard up, were better able to hide their fears and anxieties. At night, though, they were at their lowest and needed reassurance, to know that they weren't alone with their pain. She had become a nurse because she wanted to do a job that was more than just a way of earning money, and helping very ill people get through the long night made Luisa feel that she was doing something important.

Returning to her office, she did some paperwork, her capped head bent over her desk, a frown between her thin dark brows.

'I'm back from the canteen, Sister,' a cheerful voice behind her said. 'Fish pie again—I wish they'd put some fish in it! It was all potato and parsley sauce.'

Luisa could imagine it and grimaced. 'Please! You're making me feel sick!'

'Shall I tell the others to go now?' Nurse Carter asked.

'Yes, then give Mr Graham his injection, would you?'

A moment later she heard the quiet feet passing her door as her other two nurses went down to have a meal. Luisa made herself a cup of jasmine tea, a fragrant, pale golden liquid served without milk or sugar which she found refreshing during the night. She never ate in the canteen because the food was far too heavy: fatty or stolid, unimaginative. It was useless for the hospital dietitian to complain or protest. The canteen was run on a tight budget; they went for the cheapest alternative, and that was usually stodgy—bread, pasta, potatoes, often served as chips. Luisa ate fruit, nuts, yoghurt at her desk during the night, and ate her one large meal of the day at home before she came on duty each day.

The phone rang sharply in the silence, making her jump so that her pen skidded on the paper, ruining the word she had been writing. Her nerves were shot to hell tonight. Pull yourself together! she impatiently told herself, and picked up the phone. 'Burns Unit.'

'Surgical Recovery here. We're just bringing Mr West down now.'

'Right, we're ready for him.' Luisa was tidying her papers as she spoke, sliding them into a drawer in the desk and locking it.

The caller hung up. Luisa replaced her own phone and stood up, her white apron crackling. From the ward door, she could see the neatly made bed waiting for the new patient. She heard noises in the sluice-room just behind her and pushed open the door.

Anthea Carter was busy sterilising the bed pans. Flushed and faintly untidy already, she looked round, her face pinker than ever as she met Luisa's blue eyes.

'Did you want me, Sister? Sorry, Sister, I was trying to get on with these.'

'They're bringing the new patient down now, Nurse Carter. Leave that—I'll get Nurse Brett to do it when she gets back from the canteen. I want you to stay with the new admission for the rest of this shift; he's going to need constant supervision. You know how to recognise the signs of shock—

that's what we're mostly worrying about, with this one. If you see anything worrying, don't hesitate. Hit the panic button.'

Anthea Carter pulled down the bib of her apron, straightened the cap precariously perched on her curly hair. 'Yes, Sister.' She was a good nurse, in spite of her untidiness and lack of method. She was likeable, too, and Luisa smiled at her as she turned to leave.

They both heard the rattle of the lift doors. 'There they are!' Luisa said, moving to meet the new arrival. Anthea Carter deftly clipped back the swing doors so that the patient could be wheeled through into the ward by the porter pushing him, while Luisa was taking the folder of notes from the nurse who had come down with the patient. At the same time she took a quick look at the still figure being wheeled past her. He was unconscious; she winced at what she saw, but her professional training told her that in time his face could be re-built to hide the scars his burns would leave.

'Zachary West,' she murmured, looking at his notes. 'Age thirty-four. Well, Dr Hallows says he's strong and should pull through—I wonder what sort of patient he's going to be?'

'Not easy,' said the nurse who had brought him down from the theatre floor. 'I saw him when they brought him in... He was conscious for a while and made the air turn blue with his language.'

'Not unusual,' Luisa said absently, staring at the strong bone-structure of the unconscious man.

'No, but he struck me as a very angry man. If
he ever catches up with the guy who caused his accident, murder will be done.'

Luisa frowned and closed the folder of notes.
'Thank you, Nurse, you can get back to your ward
now.' She walked down the ward to oversee the
transfer of the patient from the theatre trolley to
his waiting bed, a delicate operation in his condition, although he was unconscious and could not
feel the pain which the lightest touch would
otherwise have caused him.

Once he was installed she went back to her office
to get on with her paperwork. Sometimes she
wished she hadn't been promoted: she preferred to
deal with the patients rather than sit in here doing
clerical work.

Just before dawn, Luisa did another tour of the
ward. Anthea Carter was still beside Zachary West's
bed, keeping herself busy by mending a torn hem
on one of her uniform aprons. Luisa studied his
notes. Anthea had been taking his pulse and temperature every hour; Luisa followed the line.
Nothing unexpected there.

'He hasn't shown any sign of waking up?'

'Several times I've thought...' Anthea broke off
as there was a faint movement from the bed. Their
voices must have disturbed the patient. His bruised
lids flickered upward, his eyes glistening, silvery,
unseeing, then he gave a strangled cry.

Luisa heard anguish and anger in the sound; she
bent, murmuring comfortingly, not touching him
because she knew how the lightest touch meant

agony for him, but soothing him with her low, soft voice. The wild eyes turned towards her.

'What have you done to me...?'

'We're looking after you, Mr West, don't worry.'

'Get away from me!' he snarled, and she flinched as if he had hit her.

'Give him his injection now, Nurse,' she told Anthea, standing back to watch. A moment later, the patient was asleep again, his body limp. Luisa sighed and turned away.

Back in her office she rang another ward, dialling with trembling fingers. 'Hello, Beth, it's Luisa. How is he now?'

'Fine, Luisa. Don't worry, it's just shock and a few bruises; nothing serious has developed. I expect he'll be going home today. Are you coming up to see him later?'

'Before I go home, yes.'

She replaced the phone; a tear trickled out from one eye and she angrily wiped it away.

Zachary West was trapped inside a ring of fire. Flames leapt up, glass splintered, glittering shards like daggers falling towards him. Heat seared his skin, made him blind.

I'm blind, I'm blind, I'm blind, he screamed in his dreams, but nobody heard him.

Sometimes *she* was there, floating along beside him, light as a white feather, a barn owl, a dove; a dreamlike, silent presence that calmed and soothed him. He called out to her from within his ring of fire and she slowly turned in mid-air and looked towards him. Long, wild black hair, a sweet, gentle face, dark blue eyes that held compassion and kindness. The pain fell away and Zachary sighed, holding his hands out to her.

She kept vanishing again, like a bubble bursting, and when she was not there he was plunged back into his nightmare.

Once Zachary managed to force open his eyes, cried out for her, but he didn't see her; he saw other faces, strange faces, staring down at him out of yellow light that dazzled him.

He looked angrily at them. Who were they? What had happened to the girl in white? he tried to ask, but the words wouldn't come out.

One of them bent towards him, saying something he couldn't quite hear. This one had a cold, pale face, the look of a nun. Zachary disliked her on sight, with her hair dragged back off her face, buttoned-up eyes and tight mouth. Icy, dried-up virgin.

'Where am I? What's happened?' he tried to ask, but the words came out in a mumble. He tried again, accusation in his voice. 'What have you done to me?'

She opened her mouth and said something, but he didn't hear a word; he just wanted her to go away. He told her so and she stiffened.

She said something to the other girl too quietly for him to hear, then Zachary felt a sting of pain. He glared at them: what the hell was that? What...? But they had gone, again; he was sinking back into the dreams, into the centre of the ring of fire. He wanted to scream, but he couldn't; he was trapped inside his pain. He tried to see through the flames, to look beyond to what lay outside, and suddenly she floated towards him, the girl in white, giving him that gentle smile, and Zachary's fear fell away. An angel, he thought. That's what she is—an angel! Why didn't I realise that before? I am dead, and she is an angel.

On her way home Luisa stopped off at Ward Twelve. The patients had had their breakfast and were lazily reading the morning papers or just sitting in chairs talking to each other, while the day staff got on with their morning routine. As courtesy demanded, Luisa went into the sister's office to say 'Good morning!' before she went on into the ward.

The night sister, Beth Dawlish, with whom she had trained, had hurried off long ago, and it was a woman Luisa knew only by sight who was the day sister on this ward.

'Yes, Dawlish told me you'd come by,' Sister Jacobs said, nodding, her brown eyes incurious. 'Fine by me; take your time, although I expect he'll be on his way home by this afternoon, judging by the report Dawlish left. A relief for you, anyway! It could have been much worse. How's the other one, the one you've got up on your ward? I hear he was badly injured. Car caught fire? I don't know how you can work on that ward—I did my time when I was working the wards and I hated it. You must have nerves of steel.'

Luisa managed a faint smile. 'I'm used to it. Our patient made it through the night and he's doing as well as can be expected.'

She got a dry look. 'Hmm. Like that, is it? Well, even if he pulls through he isn't out of the wood, is he? There's a long, long road ahead for him.'

'Yes,' Luisa said, shivering. 'Well, I'll let you get on...'

She walked steadily to the last bed in the ward. The man in it was sitting up against his pillows, staring at nothing, his face shadowed and white. He turned his head to look at her as she sat down on a chair beside the bed.

'Luisa...' He put out a hand, gripped her fingers so hard it hurt. 'Is...is he...?'

'Alive,' she said, her voice low and husky. 'Don't look like that. He's going to make it, Dad.'

CHAPTER TWO

LUISA slept for six hours, rather fitfully, because she had never quite got used to sleeping during the day; she finally got out of bed in the mid-afternoon, had an apple and some muesli and a cup of tea, and decided she would feel better if she got out into the fresh air and had some exercise. She was living in a small two-roomed flat within walking distance of both the hospital and Whinbury's modern shopping streets, a pedestrian precinct with paved walkways, cafés, squares and gardens.

Today was sunny and there were plenty of people about. After doing her shopping in the big supermarket in the heart of the precinct, Luisa was on her way home when she almost collided with a hurrying figure, a blonde girl not much older than herself.

'Oh, it's you!' The other girl was far from friendly; in fact her green eyes glittered with hostility.

'Hello, Noelle,' Luisa said coolly, the dislike mutual. 'Is Dad back home now?'

'Yes! And I had to go and get him; they wouldn't send him home in an ambulance!'

'The ambulance service is very overworked——' began Luisa, and the other girl interrupted furiously.

'They took him to hospital in an ambulance; why couldn't they send him back the same way? I had an important business appointment; I can't just walk out of the office whenever I like. It was very embarrassing having to cancel it; I only hope we don't lose a contract because of it. The woman who rang from the hospital was very high-handed. She insisted somebody came to get him. I couldn't see why he couldn't have come home in a taxi, or why you couldn't have brought him home. After all, you work there! It would have been no trouble to you; they said you were at home, but when I rang you all I got was your answerphone!'

'I'm on night duty; I have to sleep during the day,' Luisa said, trying not to lose her own temper, although it wasn't easy to stay calm.

'And I have to work because your father can't be bothered to run the firm any more!' retorted Noelle. 'If it wasn't for me we'd be bankrupt within a year! He has let things slide for years——'

'Never mind the firm, how's Dad?' Luisa interrupted tersely. 'You haven't left him alone, have you? He really shouldn't be alone at the moment; he's very upset.'

Noelle bristled with open resentment. 'Don't you tell me what to do! I'm not your father's secretary any more; I'm his wife, and I won't put up with you patronising me.'

'I wasn't doing anything of the kind! But I don't think you realise how dangerous shock can be... I wanted to explain the clinical——'

'Well, don't! I'm not one of your nurses, scuttling about whenever you snap your fingers!'

It wasn't pleasant to be stared at with such dislike. Luisa felt faintly sick meeting those sharp green eyes. Noelle was beautiful, there was no denying that, but for Luisa that beauty was skin-deep. From the first day they met, when Noelle joined her father's firm as his secretary, Luisa had felt uneasy. It hadn't occurred to her to suspect Noelle of being interested in her father—after all, he was a good twenty years older! No, she had simply sensed that, for some reason, Noelle did not like her, and when her father admitted to her that he was dating his secretary Luisa had been taken aback and shocked, and unable to hide it.

She should have done, of course. She wished now that she had. She bitterly wished she could like Noelle, that they could be friends, for her father's sake. She had tried hard to make friends, once she had to face the fact that the relationship was serious and was going to end in Noelle's becoming her stepmother, but it had been useless. Noelle hated her and was not prepared to come to terms.

Look at the way she was staring now, her eyes as sharp and acid as little green apples. 'As it happens, he isn't alone! Mrs North is at the house, cleaning, and I asked her to keep an eye on him. He didn't go to bed; he's lying on a couch watching television. There's nothing much wrong with him that I can see, and if he's upset he deserves it, driving like a maniac! He could have killed that man!'

Luisa paled, knowing that was true. 'But he didn't, thank God!'

'If he had it would have been your fault!' her stepmother spat, and Luisa flinched, unable to deny it. Watching her with triumph, Noelle rubbed it in, malice in every spiked syllable. 'If you hadn't rung Harry and made all that fuss he wouldn't have left the party and driven like a bat out of hell to get back home.'

Luisa's face was drawn. It was true, however much she wished it wasn't, and regrets were useless now. If she could, she would go back and change events, but you could never do that. They were strung together like beads on a string, one event leading to another inevitably. She had rung her father in a mood of wounded disappointment, and he had rushed home to placate her. If he hadn't, the accident would never have happened, and Zachary West would not be lying in a hospital bed close to death, her father would not be facing prosecution for dangerous driving ... or even worse, if Zachary West did not pull through. Ice trickled down her spine. What if he didn't ... ? No, she couldn't bear to think about that.

'But then you've always been spoilt and selfish!' Noelle said, and Luisa stared dumbly at her.

Had she? It was true that she ought to have known better than to lose her temper just because Dad had forgotten it was her birthday and had gone out with his wife, instead, but she had been so hurt, at the time. Dad had always been absent-minded; she usually had to remind him about her birthday. She saw so little of him, though, these days, that that was not so easy. She had rung a week ago to jog his memory and ask if they could have lunch, but he was out and she had had to leave a message with Noelle, which had never reached him. Instead, Noelle had lured him out to one of those long business lunches she seemed to enjoy so much. She was grimly determined to push Luisa out of her father's life, and Dad seemed blind to the battle going on over him.

Oddly enough, Luisa could see it from Noelle's point of view. It must be embarrassing to have a stepdaughter who was almost the same age as yourself; it must underline the difference in ages between man and wife, and Noelle was probably jealous, too, of the old affection Harry Gilbey had for his daughter, an affection which reminded his new wife of his dead one.

Luisa was very like her mother, as all the photographs which filled the house when she first entered it must have told Noelle. Anna Gilbey had been a graciously lovely woman of forty when she died of a heart attack, leaving her only child as a living reminder to Harry of the woman he had married when he was only twenty years old. The years since then had been lonely ones for her father. Luisa could understand why he wanted to marry again, even if his choice had astonished and disturbed her, just as she understood some of Noelle's feelings, but to understand did not make it any easier, she was to find. Luisa had always been very close to her father, especially since the death of her much-loved mother. Suddenly being cut off from him was hard to take.

Nevertheless, she had tried to accept the new situation, for Dad's sake, as much as anything. It

must be difficult for him, too, to be a buffer between two warring women, and she wanted to see
him happy again, uneasily though she viewed his
marriage to a girl of her own age.

If only she hadn't got so upset when she realised
that her father had forgotten her birthday and was
not going to be back in time to see her! But her
birthdays had always been special days: Dad had
always made them magical in the past. They had
gone out to lunch somewhere special, spent the
afternoons together, made each birthday mem-
orable. This was the first one since his marriage,
and realising that her birthday treats too were over
had hurt more than anything else so far. She had
reacted childishly when she realised where he had
gone and had rung him at the party, overwhelming
him with guilt.

No, she should never have done that—but how
could she have imagined that such disastrous consequences would flow from her outburst?

'He'll lose his licence, you know,' Noelle vindic-
tively said. 'For at least two years, the lawyer says.
And that's not the worst thing that could happen
to him. Well, I won't be able to drive him around
all the time; he'll have to get a chauffeur. He can
afford it, although he keeps saying money is tight.
He wasn't so mean when I married him. If he'd
had a chauffeur, that accident would never have
happened. At his age his judgement isn't too good
any more.'

Luisa stiffened. 'What do you mean, "at his
age"? Dad's barely fifty, for heaven's sake!'

Noelle had not apparently thought him very old when she married him! She had always been saying how young he was, how full of energy and life—and Harry Gilbey had lived up to that description over the past year, working and playing hard to keep up with his young wife. When he wasn't at cocktail parties, dinner parties, business lunches, he was out on the golf course playing with clients or people Noelle wanted him to impress.

'His reflexes aren't what they were,' shrugged Noelle.

'Maybe he goes out to parties too often! It must use up a lot of energy!' Luisa accused, and her stepmother's green eyes blazed back at her.

'That's right, shift the blame on to me! You'd love to say it was all my fault! Well, it isn't—Harry enjoys a busy social life; he always did, before he ever met me!'

Luisa couldn't deny that, either. Her father had always been a social animal; he was gregarious, lively and loved company, especially that of young people, which was no doubt why he had fallen for the ravishing blonde who had become his secretary. Noelle had encouraged him and Harry Gilbey hadn't been able to resist her and the chance to be young again.

Luisa sighed. 'Yes, I know he does.' Poor Dad. She bit her lip and looked at her stepmother with appeal in her dark blue eyes. 'Noelle, why do we always have to quarrel like this? Especially now, when Dad is in trouble...he'll need both of us over the next few months. Can't we be friends?'

Noelle's beautiful mask didn't soften. Her green eyes flashed. 'You've done enough harm, just leave us alone. Harry is my business now, not yours.' She turned to walk away, stopped, and pulled a crumpled newspaper out of the black leather briefcase she was carrying. 'Have you seen this?'

She didn't wait for an answer; she was gone a second later, leaving Luisa staring blankly at the paper, folded back to show a grey photograph of Zachary West above half a column of print headlined 'Crash Wrecks West Exhibition'.

Even more worried and depressed now, Luisa looked around for somewhere to sit down. There was a café across the square; she made for it shakily and fell into a seat near the door.

'What can I get you?' asked a waitress, coming over at once.

'Coffee, please,' Luisa said.

'Anything to eat?'

Luisa knew her blood sugar must be low; she was feeling light-headed. 'A . . . sandwich?' she muttered, glancing at the menu which stood in the centre of the red and white checked tablecloth. 'Cheese and salad sandwich, please.'

The waitress vanished and Luisa spread the newspaper out in front of her. By the time she had absorbed what it said the waitress was back with her sandwich and coffee. Luisa folded the newspaper up again with fingers that trembled, and tried to enjoy her meal, but it tasted like sawdust and ashes. All she could think about was what she had just read.

The consequences of the crash were even worse than she had imagined. Zachary West was an artist, it seemed—and famous, according to the newspaper, which had talked about large sums of money paid for his work in the past.

When the crash happened Zachary West had been taking a number of paintings up to London, in his van, to be shown in a big exhibition of his work in the gallery of a well-known art dealer. The exhibition would have been a major event in the art world, the dealer was quoted as saying. It had been awaited eagerly since Zachary West's work was much sought after and fetched increasingly large amounts and he had not exhibited his work for some years. The art world had been curious to see how he had developed his style and technique since his last exhibition. Now, said the dealer, tragically, the world would never know. All the paintings Zachary West had spent the last four years working on had been destroyed in the fire which had left the artist himself so badly burned.

Chilled and appalled, Luisa paid for her meal and left the café. She walked home and put away her shopping, then rang her father.

'How are you this afternoon, Dad?' she gently asked.

'Have you seen the newspapers?' was all he said, his voice dry and shaky.

Luisa bit her lip. 'Dad. Dad, don't——'

'Don't what?' Harry Gilbey bitterly asked her. 'Face up to what I've done? God, when I think——'

'Don't think about it, Dad, not yet. You're still shocked,' Luisa hurriedly pleaded, her blue eyes anxious.

'How can I stop thinking about it? A man like that—a genius, they say in the papers—all that talent, so much to give the world . . . and I've destroyed him . . .'

'You don't know that, Dad! He'll pull through, and he'll do other work when he's better. He's still a young man . . .' But her reassurances were only half-hearted and she knew it, because she felt just as guilty as her father, and with more reason. 'And, anyway, it's my fault, not yours,' she huskily added.

'Your fault? How can it be your fault? I was driving that car, not you!'

'But if I hadn't rung you and made so much fuss you wouldn't have been hurrying!'

'That still doesn't make it your fault, Luisa. I was the one doing the driving, and I'd been drinking—oh, I wasn't over the limit, I'm not that stupid, and I never have been a drinking man. As you know, I'm not that keen on spirits—I just had some white wine. Anyway, they breathalysed me and they said I was in the clear. But I know my reflexes were affected by the couple of drinks I'd had, my mind worked slower than it usually does, and I know in my heart that I was driving recklessly. I took the corner too fast; I was right over his side of the road . . . But that was nothing to do with you. I was in a temper—I'd had a row with Noelle—and . . . Oh, well, never mind. But it was my fault, Luisa! You mustn't blame yourself at all.'

But she did, of course, and she was still edgy and tense as she walked into the ward that evening. It was difficult to force a smile for her colleague, Mary Baker, who was Day Sister.

'Anything wrong? You don't look well,' Mary said, frowning in concern. She was a married woman with two grown-up children and had been working at the hospital for fifteen years. Easy-going and cheerful, she had been very kind during Luisa's probationary period when she worked on this ward as a very raw, anxious newcomer who had difficulty coping with what she had to do each day.

'I'm fine,' Luisa hurriedly said now, and tried to look as if it was true. Pleasant though Mary always was, Luisa still felt like a nervous probationer at times when they were talking, and she couldn't bring herself to confide in Mary. 'Just a little headache...'

'Are you sleeping properly?' Mary promptly asked, frowning. 'I don't have to remind you how vital it is to get enough sleep when you're on nights, do I?'

'No,' Luisa grimaced. 'I usually do, don't worry. So what sort of day have you had? Any new arrivals? Anyone depart?'

Mary gave her a wry look, but obligingly began to go through the ward list, putting Luisa in the picture with each patient until they came to Zachary West's name. 'He'll be going soon,' she then said, and Luisa's dark blue eyes opened wide.

'Going? What do you mean?'

'He's being whisked up to London to have specialist private nursing. It seems we've a celebrity on the ward!' Mary grinned, looking amused. 'I've been getting phone calls from Fleet Street all day, asking how he is! Would you believe some of them wanted to come up and take photos of him? He's unconscious, I said, and he doesn't look very pretty at the moment, either, so if he was conscious he wouldn't want you taking pictures of him looking like that, I told them. One or two of them turned up in person and I had to get George from the front hall to come and turf them out! Nice behaviour on a ward like this!'

'But . . . why is he leaving us?' pressed Luisa, not very interested in Fleet Street.

Mary bridled, sniffing crossly. 'Well, apparently his agent . . . or his manager, or whatever . . . doesn't think this hospital is good enough to treat such a famous man, so he wants him transferred to this London place where they specialise in skin grafts and plastic surgery. They would have taken him today, but our Mr Hallows put his foot down, told them he was in no condition to make that journey yet. It will be decided tomorrow when he'll be ready to travel, when Mr Hallows makes his round.'

Luisa was appalled. 'I wouldn't have thought it was possible for him to bear that trip to London! It would be so painful for him.'

He was being fed intravenously and kept on continuous medication in order to get him over these first few days with as little pain as possible. Luisa stood beside him, staring at the grim mask he would show the world for many months to come, until he was fit enough for plastic surgery. From the photo she had seen of him, in the newspaper, he must have been an attractive man. It was terrible to see him the way he was now.

As Mary had said earlier, thank heavens he was physically strong. Otherwise he could never have survived that crash, or already begun to show the first faint signs of a recovery.

As it was, you could see that he was a powerfully built, lean man with slim hips and long legs and the muscles of someone used to exercise—or, perhaps, to constant work. His lower body had escaped the worst of the fire; his legs were almost unscathed, their skin tanned and dusted with dark hairs.

Suddenly his lids flicked up and she found herself looking into his eyes, pale eyes like polished silver, his enlarged black pupils dominating his gaze, a sure sign to her of the drugs they were having to give him to damp down his pain.

Luisa's professionalism took over and she bent hurriedly towards him, smiling reassurance.

'Hello, how are you feeling now?'

Zachary West didn't even try to answer. He vaguely remembered her and his scorched brows drew together painfully. This was the pale, cold woman he had seen standing beside his bed before, although he couldn't quite be sure how long ago that was.

But then time had become a labyrinth through which he endlessly searched for a way out. He didn't know how long he had been like this; he only knew that he kept waking up and going back to sleep and the moments in between were brief and painful, almost surreal. Each time he couldn't think where he was or what had happened to him, and each time the pain was lurking to spring out at him. He always escaped from consciousness with a sense of relief because when he was awake everything hurt, although he couldn't quite recall why. All he knew was that his life had simply stopped suddenly one day when he was driving along a road, and ever since he had been in pain.

'I'm Sister Gilbey,' the woman said. 'I'm looking after you, Mr West. How do you feel?'

She had a soft, low voice that should have soothed. Instead, he was irritated by it. Did she think he was a child?

Zachary swallowed and became aware of a raging thirst. 'Drink...' he tried to say through his dry lips, and she must have understood because she gently inserted a straw between his teeth. He sucked weakly, and cool water came into his mouth. He stopped sucking when he had quenched his thirst, and his eyes closed in weariness.

'Are you in much pain?' the woman asked stupidly.

Zachary opened his eyes to look at her with contempt. What did she think? his gaze asked her.

He closed his eyes again and very soon he was slipping back into his dream. The girl was waiting with her windblown black hair and glimmering oval face, the smile that made his blood sing. Zachary floated towards her, smiling, his heart beating faster.

When his surgeon saw him again the following day Zachary was awake for the first time and David Hallows was able to talk to him.

'Your agent, Mr Curtney, wants you to be moved up to London to another hospital which specialises in skin conditions, but I'm afraid . . . although you are already much improved and I have every faith that you will go on improving very fast . . . for the moment I'm afraid I cannot really permit you to make such a long journey.'

Zachary West gazed incuriously at him, his body slack. 'I see.'

He did not seem too disturbed by the news and David Hallows gave him a friendly, encouraging smile.

'We'll take the best possible care of you, Mr West. We're trying to make you comfortable.'

'I've been too drugged to notice,' Zachary said suddenly, his voice clearer than it had been since his accident.

David Hallows laughed. 'Well, yes, that was necessary for the first few days, to protect you against too much movement, and to counter the effects of shock. From now on we will be cutting back on the dosage; we don't want you getting hooked, do we?'

He laughed again. Zachary didn't. Bleakly he said, 'There's no chance of that. I hate being out of my mind.'

'Quite,' David Hallows said. 'Well, I'm happy to see you recovering so rapidly. I'll be in to see you again tomorrow, a little earlier as it's Saturday. Keep your fingers crossed that I get a quiet weekend for once!'

Again he laughed, and this time Zachary showed a spark of amusement in his grey eyes.

'That might be a little difficult for me at present.'

David did a double take, then grinned in some surprise. 'Yes, I'm afraid you're right.' Zachary's hands had been very badly burned and must be intensely painful.

Talking to Luisa that evening, David said, 'I have a lot of respect for the man; he's got guts. I've known men with burns that weren't half as bad as his who made ten times the fuss. To be making jokes this early shows a very strong character. I don't think I'd be that brave if I were in his place.' He grimaced. 'In fact, I know I wouldn't be! I'm petrified of having his sort of injuries. That's probably why I specialised in skin surgery. My father was badly burnt in an explosion in a chemical works when I was ten, and I've never forgotten seeing him a week or so later. I had nightmares for years afterwards, kept dreaming it was me under the bandages.'

Luisa looked fixedly at him, her blue eyes as dark as gentians in the shadowy light of her office. 'Poor David, how frightening it must have been for you at such an early age.' He had never told her this story before and it revealed a lot about him that she had never suspected.

A little flushed, he laughed and got up, shrugging. 'Yes...well...I must go. I'm going home now. I've run out of bodies in the theatre so I might as well get some sleep. See you tomorrow. Looking forward to it?'

Luisa lit up, smiling. 'Oh, yes. I haven't been to a dance for ages and I love dancing. I'm going to buy a new dress tomorrow, too!'

'To go out with me? I'm flattered!' He grinned down at her, a head taller than her, his attractive face warm, yet still set in lines of exhaustion and weariness.

Luisa didn't manage to get out to do her shopping until quite late on Saturday afternoon, but there was only one good dress shop in Whinbury so she would not need much time in which to make her choice. She was lucky: there was a ravishing dark blue silk dress with a low-cut bodice and a stand-up ruff of lace at the back. The dress was long-skirted with a trio of rustling pale pink lace petti-coats under it, and a pale pink silk rose pinned to the waist. Luisa loved the feel of the frou-frou of petticoats around her legs as she walked.

'It has a sort of Victorian look, doesn't it?' said the girl who sold it to her. 'Your hairstyle goes with it. Very classy, that chignon. Of course some of them wore ringlets in Victorian days, too, but I think that was the young girls, not ladies of your age.'

Luisa laughed without amusement. The girl was probably not even twenty; no doubt to her Luisa's twenty-seven years did seem pretty ancient, but it left Luisa feeling as if she had suddenly aged without noticing it. Twenty-seven wasn't that old! Why shouldn't she wear her hair in ringlets if she liked? Victorian, indeed!

When she got home she had a bath, washed her hair, and spent some time curling it into Victorian-style ringlets with some electric hair tongs she had once been given, but rarely used.

Once she was dressed for the dance she stood in front of her mirror, biting her lip. The new style certainly made her look different! In fact, it changed her whole appearance. She went pink. What on earth had she done to herself? She felt ridiculous and would have tried to restore her hair to normal if David hadn't arrived while she was still trying to make up her mind what to do.

He did a double take, staring. 'Luisa? Good heavens! I hardly recognised you. Your hair...'

Luisa groaned. 'It looks awful, doesn't it? I don't know what on earth made me do it! But——'

'I love it!'

She blinked uncertainly. 'You do?'

'It's perfect with that dress.' He held out his well-shaped hand, his brown eyes warm. 'And that is a very sexy dress, let me say!'

She laughed, but went pink, and David smiled down at her, holding her slender fingers lightly. 'The blush is sexy, too.'

'Don't you make fun of me, David Hallows!' she protested, even more flushed.

'I'm not, I mean it. When you go pink like that you look very female. I suppose it makes me feel you need protecting...'

'In this day and age?' she asked incredulously.

He grimaced. 'Oh, I know it's an out of date attitude—opening doors for a woman, standing up when she comes into a room...OK, it's laughed at these days. But I'm an old-fashioned guy. I like the difference between a man and a woman and I don't see why I should apologise for that.'

'Neither do I,' she said, smiling at him because they had worked together long enough for her to know that he was no put-down artist. He didn't treat women as dolls—far from it. He'd always treated her with respect and grave equality.

He smiled back. 'That's what first attracted me to you,' he surprised her by saying. 'Your femininity.'

Luisa stared in surprise. He had never told her that before. She had often wondered how he had managed to reach the age of thirty-five without marrying because he was attractive and popular with the other nurses. He had had other girl-friends, but the relationships had all fizzled out in the end. Maybe the long hours he had to work, the intense concentration of the job, always came between him and anyone he dated?

He usually looked relaxed and casual, even in his ward-walking suits, because he was not the authoritarian type of surgeon of an earlier gener-ation. David was too laid-back for that; his warm smile and easy-going manner made him the most liked of all the doctors. But tonight he, too, looked different: very distinguished in his evening suit. The black jacket and trousers made him look very slim; the white shirt and immaculate black tie gave him a touch of glamour he did not normally have.

His mouth curled in amusement. 'Are you looking me over, Luisa? Or have I put you off by admitting I like feminine girls?'

She laughed, shaking her head.

He tightened his grip on her hand and drew her closer, bending his head. Luisa instinctively lifted her face to meet his kiss, but, even as their lips met, behind them in her flat the telephone rang and they froze, looked at each other, grimacing.

'Don't answer it!' David said, and she laughed.

'You know I must! It may be my father.'

David groaned. 'Famous last words!'

It wasn't her father; it was the hospital. She sighed and turned, holding out the phone to David. 'Sorry,' she said as he reluctantly took it.

'I won't say I told you so!'

He curtly said into the phone, 'Hallows here.' Then listened, brows pulling together. 'How long has that been happening?'

Luisa stood watching him, her hands unconsciously playing with her short black velvet evening jacket. If David was being summoned back to the theatre she would not be going to the dance.

He put the phone down and turned to make a wry face at her. 'I told you not to answer it!'

'I thought you weren't on call!'

'I'm not, but one of my patients has been waiting for an op. for three days because his condition simply wasn't stable enough for me to risk it. Tonight they think he has stabilised, but Colin Dawkins doesn't like to risk doing an op. on his own opinion; he wants me to pop in and take a look at the guy and back him up before he gives the go-ahead.'

'And he'd really rather you did the op. yourself!' Luisa said drily.

David laughed. 'I expect he would. He's simply terrified of taking a risk, that fellow.'

'Does this mean no dance?'

'Certainly not! No, we'll be going, but I suppose I'd better make a detour *en route* and drop by the hospital to see this patient and decide whether Colin ought to operate or not.'

'It might be wiser to wait until tomorrow, anyway.'

David's mouth indented. 'Hmm. This is a dodgy one, though. Not sure he can afford to wait. But I'll see.'

When they reached the hospital David asked, 'Wait here for me?' but she shook her head, smiling at him.

'You may be gone for ages. No, I'll come in and stop off at my ward to have a cup of coffee with Sister Jenkins.'

'And show off your dress?' he teased, and she laughed.

'Well, why not?'

They split up in the hospital, and she rustled along the corridors, amused when she got a startled look from a nurse hurrying by.

Helen Jenkins was in the ward overseeing a nurse giving out the evening medication. Luisa walked towards them and Helen looked round, and stared, open-mouthed.

'Can't you keep away?'

Laughing, Luisa explained. 'David had to see a patient. I hoped I'd get a cup of coffee from you while I wait.'

'Put it on and I'll be with you in a second,' Helen cheerfully agreed.

'What a gorgeous, dress, Sister,' said the nurse, and Luisa smiled at her.

'Thanks, it's new. First time I've worn it.'

'It suits you,' said the girl, her eyes lifting to stare at Luisa's ringlets.

Helen was staring at them, too. 'I've never seen you wear your hair like that before!'

'I never have; it's an experiment, and I don't think I'll be doing it again, either,' Luisa wryly said.

'Oh, no, it looks great!' the nurse said, and Helen nodded.

'I like it, too. It certainly makes you look different.'

Rather pink, Luisa said, 'Thank you,' and then turned to walk back to the office. As she did so, a faint voice made her halt. She looked across the ward at Zachary West's bed and saw him shift slightly. Luisa went over to him. His eyes were open.

'Did you call out, Mr West?'

He stared in silence.

She tried again. 'I thought I heard you call...'

He closed his eyes without answering.

'I'm seeing things now!' he muttered to himself, and she had to bend closer to hear the words. 'Crazy!' he was murmuring barely audibly, through his swollen lips. 'I'm going crazy! God help me.'

His eyes opened again suddenly. He gave a start, finding her so near. Luisa gave him what she hoped was a soothing smile. 'Is there anything I can get you, Mr West?'

All she got back was a ferocious look and a snarl. 'Go away, for God's sake! I can't take any more! Go away!'

She was so taken aback that without another word she obeyed, her skirts rustling as she hurried towards the office.

To her horror, her blue eyes had filled with tears. What is the matter with me? she wondered and fumbled for a paper tissue to angrily wipe her wet eyes. He can't help being bad-tempered; he's very ill! He isn't the first patient to turn on you, heaven knows! Why are you weeping over him?

She began to make the coffee, as Helen Jenkins had asked, but she never had a chance to drink it because just as Helen joined her the phone rang. It was David.

'Ready?'

'Yes, of course,' she said, furious to realise that her voice was still husky. 'How was your patient?'

'Not yet up to an op. See you at the car in two minutes!'

She put down the phone and turned. 'Sorry, Nell, David didn't take as long as I'd expected. See you later tonight.'

'Yes. Have a wonderful time, but don't be late back!' Helen said, grinning at her.

On her way out of the ward Luisa paused for one second to look down the ward towards Zachary West. He seemed to have gone back to sleep now. She sighed and hurried away to find David.

As they had both realised it would, their arrival together at the hospital dinner-dance in Whinbury's best hotel made something of a stir. Everyone had known they were going out together, but for them to come to such a very important event together was seen as some sort of declaration of intent. They were now publicly an admitted pair.

'When you come to choose your bridesmaids think of me!' one of her friends said in the ladies' cloakroom during the evening.

Luisa pulled an impatient face at her. 'Give us a chance, Jane! We've only been going out for a few months. Marriage isn't on our minds.'

'Bet I know what is!' Jane Dorset said, giggling. 'Well, on his, anyway! I've seen the way he looks at you.'

Luisa blushed, which made everyone hoot with laughter. Not for the first time she furiously wished she didn't colour up so easily. David might find it charmingly feminine, but it was a curse Luisa could do without.

David drove her back to the hospital at half-past one when the dance ended. 'Enjoy yourself?' he asked after switching off his engine in the car park.

Luisa nodded, eyes bright. 'I had a wonderful time, David. Thank you, it was terrific. I only wish I didn't have to go back to work!'

After eating a four-course meal which included a very rich roast duck with cherries and a chocolate and orange mousse, drinking champagne, laughing and talking to friends and dancing with David to a very good band for several hours, she was in no mood to change back into her uniform and put in a six-hour shift.

'So do I, believe me. If you had the rest of the night off we could get to know each other better...' David softly said, and her maddening colour flowed up her face again, making him smile. 'You're so lovely, Luisa,' he muttered, his fingers gently stroking her cheek and then sliding down to tilt her head back.

Their lips met and Luisa closed her eyes. Yet somehow she couldn't give herself to David's passionate mouth. Some part of her was cool, resistant; her body arched away from him although she didn't push him away.

After a moment he lifted his head and looked wryly at her. 'I picked the wrong moment, didn't I?'

'I'm sorry, David, I'm just not in that mood any more... I suppose it's having to go back to work right away...' she whispered guiltily.

He gave her a comforting smile. 'Never mind, there'll be other times. You had better hurry in and change. Goodnight, Luisa.'

As soon as she had changed back into uniform and Helen Jenkins had gone, Luisa went down the ward to Zachary West's bed.

He was asleep. She stood watching him, wishing she understood the strange, driving compulsion to see him which had possessed her all evening while she talked, laughed, ate, danced. Her body had been with David, but her mind had been here, with this strange, hostile, aggressive man towards whom she felt such complicated responses.

After a few moments she went on around the ward to check on all her other patients, then back to her office to get on with her work there, but every so often she would pause, glance up, and stare down towards Zachary West, then sigh and look down again, bewildered by her own feelings.

Zachary West was in her ward throughout the following week, a little better each day, waiting for David to agree that he was strong enough to make the journey to London to the specialist hospital. Luisa wished David would agree. She would feel easier if Zachary West were not around.

Or would she? She wanted him gone, but she felt oddly low whenever the time came round for David to make the decision, and each time she came on duty in the evening and found Zachary West still there she felt something disturbingly like relief.

Twelve days after the accident, though, she walked into the ward one night and there was another patient in Zachary West's bed. He had gone.

Luisa stood staring down the ward, a wave of coldness sweeping over her, then she shook herself and turned away. Thank heavens, now she could get back to her own life and forget all about Zachary West.

CHAPTER THREE

IT WAS months before Luisa heard of Zachary West
again, although she thought of him from time to
time, always at moments when she wasn't expecting to, as if he hid inside her mind and leapt
out at her while she was busy thinking about something else.

Each time it was a shock: her nerves would jump
and her heart turn over.

She could have understood it if she was in love
with the man, but she didn't even like him. He had
not been a good patient and she instinctively knew
that even if he had been in perfect health he would
have been curt, offhand, indifferent. The photo of
him she had seen in a newspaper had told her that
much. He wasn't an easy man to like, judging by
what she had read about him and seen in his face
in that photograph.

She didn't know why she should find him so hard
to forget. It irritated her.

Her father never mentioned him, or the accident. The case hadn't come up in court yet; there
was apparently a huge backlog of accident cases
and until he was given notice that he must attend
the court Harry Gilbey preferred to forget all about
it. Luisa could understand that. So did she. Why
couldn't she?

She was seeing David whenever either of them had any free time. Which meant not often. Their jobs saw to that. She could see why David had never married. When would he have found the time? Work obsessed him; he talked of it when he wasn't doing it, and when he was he had an air of cheerful concentration which made him impervious to everything else.

Luisa didn't mind, however. Their calm, affectionate relationship satisfied her. It suited her as much as it suited David. She did not want a wild, passionate love-affair. David's gentleness and common sense was what she was looking for in a man.

Which made it all the stranger that she could not get Zachary West out of her head. He was not the calm and reasonable type of man she preferred.

He was elemental: like the wind howling over moorland, or the crack of thunder following a flash of lightning. You couldn't predict it or control it. Luisa had always been afraid of thunderstorms, and hated the sound of a high wind. Zachary West disturbed and alarmed her, in just the same way.

Just before Christmas that year, her father rang her at home one afternoon not long after she had got out of bed. 'I hope I didn't wake you? Are you working tonight, or could we meet for dinner? I haven't seen much of you lately; we must talk about Christmas, Luisa. What are your plans?'

'I'm working on Christmas Day itself, but I do have a couple of days off after that.' She hadn't raised the subject with her father because she suspected Noelle wouldn't want her around over the holiday and she didn't want to embarrass her father by making it necessary for him to tell her so.

'Right,' he said slowly. 'Well, when can we meet to talk about it?'

'Tonight? I'm not working.'

'Then how about dinner at the Cherry Tree?'

'That would be lovely.' It was Whinbury's newest restaurant; she had been there with David a few weeks earlier and had enjoyed the food enormously. 'It's just a few minutes from here; I can walk there and meet you in the restaurant.'

'Fine, there will just be us,' Harry Gilbey said casually, and Luisa's mouth curved in wry understanding. He meant that Noelle wouldn't be there. Luisa wasn't surprised. She knew that her stepmother avoided her company as much as possible, and she felt much the same. She was relieved to be told that she wouldn't have to face Noelle's hostile gaze, but she tried to keep her voice neutral.

'What time shall I arrive, Dad?'

'Seven-thirty?'

'Great. I'll be there.'

She put on a dress she knew her father liked, a blue lambswool dress in a simple, long-sleeved, polo-neck style which clung to her, however, emphasising the curve of her slim figure.

He was waiting when she arrived, a man of much the same height as herself, slim-hipped, and very fit because he still played squash and tennis, and swam every day, although his hair was turning grey at his temples, she suddenly saw.

His suit was very much a young man's suit, absolutely up to the latest style, and so were his shirt and tie, his casual shoes. If you took a quick look as you passed you might have been fooled. You had to look again to see that under the street-smart dress was the body of a man of fifty.

She felt a pang of sadness. Why was it so vital to him to stay young? He was her father and she loved him, which made it hurt her to see him fighting a losing battle with such terrible intensity. It wasn't just his clothes; they weren't important. It was his painful desire not to act or look his real age that hurt.

He stood up and kissed her. 'You look very pretty, darling.'

'Thank you, you look very good yourself, Dad.' It wasn't absolutely true. His face was beginning to show lines of worry and exhaustion. Since his accident he really was starting to show his age.

'Thanks, Luisa.' His smile was strained, though. 'Shall we go to the table, or have a drink at the bar?'

'Let's have a drink first,' she said easily, hoping to get him to unwind a little. Was he usually this tense now, or had something else happened lately?

He had a glass of whisky. She drank white wine. The waiter brought them menus and they read them while they sipped their drinks.

After they had ordered, her father said, 'Luisa, the reason I wanted to talk to you...about Christmas...well, the thing is...' He was flushed and couldn't meet her eyes, and she stiffened, suddenly realising what he was going to say.

'Noelle doesn't want me there?' The words emerged from her throat rawly, as painfully as talking through a mouthful of razor blades.

Her father winced. 'It isn't that, darling!'

She laughed. 'Oh, let's be honest, Dad. Noelle wishes I'd just vanish, and maybe that's what I should do. It might make your life easier if I did.'

'It would make me miserable,' he said harshly. 'Don't talk like that, Luisa!'

She put a hand over his. 'I'm sorry, Dad. Forget I said it. Don't worry about me. I'll probably have to work, anyway. You know how it is at Christmas—we always seem to be even busier over that week.'

What was the point in making things harder for him? He had fallen in love with a girl half his age and married her, and now he was having to face the consequences. Noelle was relentless. She wouldn't share him with his daughter, who might remind him of his dead first wife. She wanted Luisa out of their lives, and she was determined to have her own way. Harry Gilbey couldn't stand up to her. He was too nice a man. He wanted life to be pleasant, not one long battleground; whenever Noelle began a fight he let her win. It was crazy, of course. The more he gave in, the more ruthless she became. But he couldn't help himself; Luisa could see that. That was his nature, and Noelle exploited it.

He sighed. 'We used to have great Christmases, though.'

'Yes, didn't we?' Luisa sighed, too.

They both sat in silence for a while, then Harry
Gilbey said, 'You see, the thing is . . . Noelle wants
to go abroad, to Switzerland, for Christmas. She's
heard of a wonderful hotel from some friends of
hers. They're going, too. We could have Christmas
and ski if there's snow.'

'Sounds fabulous.' Luisa was sincere about that.
She and her father had often taken skiing holidays
in Austria and Switzerland, and she loved both the
scenery and the sport, not to mention the après-ski
social life.

'Yes, if only. . . I wish you could come too, but. . .'

'Some other time, Dad,' she said, trying to sound
cheerful.

The waiter approached, smiling. 'Your table is
ready, sir.'

As they walked towards the table Luisa changed
the subject, began to talk about a new patient on
her ward, a very autocratic old lady who was
making their lives impossible.

'And then she said to Anthea Carter, "My
internal workings are none of your business, young
lady, and I'm not answering any more of your im-
pertinent questions." So Anthea said, "Well, you
won't have your operation until you do!" and Mrs
Abbot's face was a picture.'

Mr Gilbey laughed, his face softening. 'Is her op.
serious?'

'No, a minor one, and she'll be fine; she's as
tough as old boots, and David is a brilliant surgeon.'

Her father gave her a quick, searching look. 'Is
it serious, darling? You and David?'

She blushed, her smooth translucent skin filling with hot blood.

Her father laughed. 'Does that mean yes—or no?'

'I like him a lot, but we aren't talking about marriage, if that's what you mean—at least, not yet.'

'Which of you isn't sure?' he asked, watching her and trying to read her expression. He was sure Luisa was in love; there was something different about her although he couldn't quite put his finger on it. There had been a darker blue to her eyes lately, a faintly wistful line to her mouth.

Harry Gilbey felt a tingle of antagonism towards David Hallows. If he hurts my girl I'll kill him! he thought.

But Luisa laughed, her face wry. 'We're just too busy to think about it. We both have careers that matter more than anything else just now. Maybe one day. But not yet.'

He frowned. 'I know you're serious about your profession, but you can go on with that and still get married! Don't you want children, Luisa? You get on with them so well; I'd have sworn you'd love some.'

'I would,' she agreed, her mouth taking that wistful line again. 'But . . . well, I don't know . . . it doesn't seem urgent to get married and have children yet, if you know what I mean?'

'Maybe David isn't the right man for you?' her father thought aloud. 'When you fall in love with the right man you'll know, and then you'll want to marry as soon as possible and start a family.'

She looked at him across the table, laughing. 'Oh, Dad! That's the most antiquated attitude! Women have careers now; they can take care of themselves. They don't need to get married to find a man to take care of them any more!'

'But they still need love,' he sighed, then his face clouded over. He was thinking of Noelle, realised Luisa, watching him with sympathy.

The waiter came and whisked their first course away, and refilled their wine glasses.

'Now, what do you want for Christmas, Luisa?' her father asked, and she relaxed, supposing that from now on they could just enjoy themselves and forget all their problems.

It wasn't until they were leaving the restaurant an hour later that Harry Gilbey blurted out what she afterwards realised must have been weighing on his mind all evening.

'My court case is scheduled at last, by the way.'

She swung to face him, pale-faced in the amber light of the streetlamp. 'When?'

'Late January.'

'It's taken all this time!'

He grimaced, trying to make light of it. 'Crazy, isn't it?'

'It seems cruel to me. Making people wait so long, when they're dreading what's in store for them.'

He sighed. 'Yes. It happened last spring, you know, the accident. It has been a bad year. Well, thank goodness I passed the breathalyser test. It would have been ten times more serious if I'd been drunk.'

She looked anxiously at him. 'What does your lawyer say your chances are? What could happen?'

He shrugged. 'I could lose my licence for good, or for two or three years. I could pay a hefty fine. He says it's hard to guess. Depends on the court.' He paused, looking at his watch. 'I'll walk you back to your flat and ring from there for a taxi, if you don't mind.'

'Of course not.' They started to walk and she asked, 'Is that how you're getting around now? By taxi?'

He nodded. 'I haven't driven since the accident, and I don't imagine I ever will drive again. I have that man's terrible injuries on my conscience—I ruined his life.'

'You can't possibly know, Dad! He has probably had plastic surgery by now and could be well on the way to recovery. His burns weren't as bad as some I've seen. They were only twenty per cent——'

'Isn't that bad enough, for heaven's sake?'

'Of course, but you didn't intend it to happen. It was an accident!'

He wasn't listening to her, his eyes haunted. 'And I destroyed all those paintings. He's a famous artist, and they were his best work to date, canvases he had been working on for years...all gone up in smoke. How he must hate me.'

'I'm sure he doesn't; he must realise it was an accident! Stop torturing yourself!'

A groan wrenched out of him. 'You don't understand, you don't know... Luisa, I've got to tell you; I have to tell someone...I dare not tell Noelle;

she would go crazy. I shudder to think what she'll
do when she does find out, and she will, once the
case comes to court.'

He looked hag-ridden. Luisa slid her arm through
his and squeezed his arm reassuringly as they
reached her flat. 'I'm sure it can't be as bad as you
think, whatever it is. Look, come in and have a
coffee and we'll talk it over.'

He nodded and from his face she could see that
that was what he needed—to confide in someone
who would try to understand. He followed her up
to her flat. First of all she turned on the electric
fire, to give the room a welcoming feel. There was
central heating, but it was only a background heat;
on cold nights you needed a fire, too. She then went
into the kitchen alcove off the sitting-room to make
the coffee while her father stood staring at the red
glow of the electric bars.

She made coffee and brought the tray across to
the low coffee-table in front of the fire. 'Sit down,
Dad, and drink your coffee in comfort.'

He obediently sat, like a child, in one of her arm-
chairs, clasping his cup in both hands as if he was
very chilled.

'Now, tell me the problem,' she urged, smiling.
She imagined he was going to tell her yet again that
he knew he had caused the accident.

What he actually said was, 'I had forgotten to
pay my insurance.'

'What?' she asked stupidly.

'It had lapsed and I kept meaning to send the
cheque to renew it, but I kept forgetting,' her father
expanded.

'Oh, my God,' Luisa said, beginning to realise what this would mean. She was white, and felt very cold.

'And if the court finds that I was responsible for the accident I'll have to pay the whole sum myself,' Harry Gilbey said shakily.

She gazed at him, too numb to speak, and he nodded grimly at her.

'Zachary West will sue me for every penny I have in the world, Luisa!'

'Oh, Dad!' she breathed, horrified.

'And when Noelle finds out, she'll leave me,' he muttered.

'Of course she won't!' Luisa protested, although she secretly thought he might well be right. She believed Noelle had married him because he had money, and if he lost it Noelle might leave. Frowning, Luisa asked, 'But surely the court will give you plenty of time to pay? They won't force you to pay at once!'

'They probably won't, but...you see, I've already got a mortgage on the house. I needed money in a hurry—to pay for that honeymoon... She wanted a world trip, and it was wonderful, but it cost a lot. And then she wanted her own car, and that was reasonable, wasn't it?'

'A Porsche, isn't it?' Luisa drily asked.

He met his daughter's eyes and flushed. 'Well, she's sensitive about having been my secretary; she felt she had to make people realise that things were different now. She had to have new clothes, and she couldn't go on driving that clapped-out old banger.'

Luisa thought of the designer fashion she had noticed Noelle wearing since the marriage. Noelle loved expensive things. It was a thrill to her to spend lots of money, since she had never had much. If Dad had really been rich that wouldn't have mattered; he had enjoyed giving his new wife everything she wanted. But if he had had to borrow the money to pay for her extravagance that changed everything! Did Noelle know?

'And I had expenses with the company,' Harry Gilbey abruptly went on. 'We had the new annexe built to the factory, when we got that Spanish contract—we had to, Luisa! Noelle was right—you expand or you stagnate. So I borrowed against the factory, too. To pay for the alterations.'

'How much?' Luisa asked with dread.

He paused, swallowing, then blurted out, 'A quarter of a million.'

She shut her eyes. 'Dad.'

He groaned again. 'I know. I've been a fool.'

Luisa looked at him then and smiled wryly. 'No, Dad, you were just in love, and Noelle is beautiful.'

He gave her a gratified look. 'Yes, she is. And she's clever, you know. She did have brilliant ideas for the business—she said it had been run down and we had to modernise or go under. I suppose she was right—I haven't given enough attention to the firm since your mother died. It has just been ticking over for years. The factory was shabby and we hadn't updated the department store at all. Since Noelle took over, all that has changed.'

'But if you have to pay heavy damages to Zachary West you're going to be saddled with an enormous debt for years!' Luisa thought aloud.

'I simply couldn't pay it,' he flatly said. 'When I took out the first mortgage it wasn't so bad, but with the two mortgages... I can barely pay them both now. And at my age, I could only get a short-term loan, for ten years, which meant high interest rates, of course.'

She flinched at the thought of what those interest rates must be. 'How much is left to repay?'

'Most of it,' he said flatly. 'If I have to pay huge damages to Zachary West the house will have to go. Maybe even the business. It depends how much the court fixes the damages at, and how long they give me to pay them.'

Appalled, Luisa stared at him. 'Is it that bad? But surely...ours is such an old-established firm... The bank will lend you enough to tide you over!'

'Not when I already have two other mortgages. Oh, if I hadn't had the accident I'd have repaid the mortgages out of profits. We are already doing much more business—Noelle has turned the firm around, pushed our income right up.' He gave Luisa an almost pleading look. 'She was right, you see! If only we had had better luck. It's the accident that has wrecked everything.'

When he had gone Luisa sat staring into the electric fire, her lower lip caught between her teeth. That accident had done irreparable damage to all of them. And it had been her fault.

Oh, her father still wouldn't let her say so, but she knew it had been her fault. If she hadn't behaved like a whiny child . . .

If only there were something she could do to help him, to make up for what she had caused! But she had no money, apart from a small amount she had saved towards her holidays next year. Far too small to be of any use to her father.

Zachary West wasn't the type to be generous, either, or ready to forgive. She shivered, remembering his hostile eyes, the face she had seen in that newspaper photograph. He was a hard man.

But if he realised the ruin he would inflict on her father's life? Would he be prepared to come to some arrangement?

She went to bed in a depressed mood, but slept well, no doubt because of the wine she had drunk over dinner. Next morning she got up early and had fruit for breakfast, then took down the telephone directory and looked up Zachary West.

At least she could be sure that there was only one Zachary West! His address was: Captain's Cottage, Tareton Road, Tareton. She knew the village—it was only half an hour from town. But first she pulled the phone towards her and began dialling Zachary West's number without giving herself time to get cold feet.

The ringing went on and on, and Luisa was about to hang up when somebody picked up the phone at the other end.

A harsh voice snarled, 'Yes?' and her nerves jumped. It was him. She knew that hostile tone.

Luisa put the phone down without answering. Well, now she knew that he was at the cottage.

She put a short cherry-red wool jacket over her white sweater and black trousers and went out to her car, a two-year-old red Mini she had bought herself that summer instead of taking a holiday abroad.

Within a short time the town petered out and she was driving along narrow coastal roads with the sea on her left, and on her right fields still veiled in drifting sea mist. The trees were bare, the ploughed fields full of gulls which had come inland to flee from winter storms at sea.

She drove through the village of Tareton which was far from busy at this time of year. In summer when there were tourists around it was often crowded, but not in December.

She found Zachary West's isolated red-bricked Queen Anne cottage about a mile further on, set back from the road in a walled garden. The cottage was perched on the cliff top above a sea-lashed bay and as Luisa drew up outside the gate she could well imagine the wind howling around it on a stormy night.

There were no other houses within sight, just acres of flat fields, some of which held grazing sheep feeding on chopped root vegetables spread for them by a farmer on a tractor. You couldn't imagine a lonelier place. Most people would find it grim, but somehow it suited what she remembered of Zachary West.

Crows which had been sitting on a rowan tree in the garden flapped raggedly away like torn black handkerchiefs as Luisa got out of the car.

As if their flight had been some sort of alarm, she heard footsteps on the old brick path running around the house and then Zachary West himself came into sight, staring towards the gate.

Luisa had just opened it and froze there, staring back at him.

'Who are you? What do you want?' he grated, scowling, the wind whipping his black hair back from his temples. His hair had grown again, thick and long, giving him a wild look.

She could see that he had had some plastic surgery, but his face still showed signs of the accident: his scarred skin livid, a dead white colour surrounding the discoloured marks. He would have to undergo further surgery, obviously. She knew that a good surgeon didn't do too much in one session, but liked to give the body time to cope with each new operation.

Luisa noted his condition professionally, used to faces like his, but aware that someone who wasn't used to such sights might well be horrified by the sight of him.

Her silence probably made Zachary West think that she was struck dumb by horror, too.

His lip curled back, giving him the appearance of a snarling wolf. 'Oh, go away!' he threw at her, turning away, and she had a sense of *déjà vu* for a second, recalling the night when she had visited his bedside in her evening dress.

'Go away!' he had told her then, and for some inexplicable reason the furious dismissal had brought tears to her eyes.

This time her reaction was as instinctive, but different. He knew how he looked and he hated other people to see him like this! She felt his pain as if it were her own and a wave of pity flooded through her.

'Don't you remember me, Mr West?' she quietly said, and he stopped, turned, stared at her with narrowed eyes.

'Should I?' The question was insulting, the way he looked her up and down deliberate, but she didn't colour or flinch. She gazed back at him mildly, her blue eyes grave.

'I'm Sister Gilbey, from Whinbury Hospital. I nursed you for a week immediately after your accident.'

He stared harder, then shrugged. His voice curt, he said, 'Did you? I don't remember much about that time.'

'You were very ill,' she agreed.

'Yes, I do remember that.' His voice was ironic now. He was mocking her, and she sighed. It wasn't going to be easy to talk to this man. What on earth had made her think it would be? What had convinced her that she could persuade him to be generous and reasonable with her father?

Then she looked into his eyes and the angry pride she saw there made her forget her own worries for a moment.

'You look much better now,' she said gently, and he laughed, his grey eyes almost black with bitter rage.

'Oh, do I?' He took two long strides back towards her, towering over her and making her realise for the first time how very tall he was, how physically dominating with those broad shoulders, that muscled body and long legs.

Luisa was slightly built, her head only came up to his shoulder, and she felt herself tremble in front of the threat of his strength.

Startled, she flickered a glance up at him, instinctively taking a step backwards. 'Y-yes, you do look much better...' she stammered, and he bared his white teeth in a wolfish grin.

'Handsome, am I? The first time you saw me just now I could see I'd knocked your eyes out— you were quite breathless with excitement. Couldn't get a word out, you were so struck by my good looks.'

He caught hold of her arms, his fingers biting into her flesh, and Luisa's nerves leapt in panic.

'Mr West, please...'

He pulled her even closer, his hold on her relentless.

'No need to beg—I'm going to give you what you want!'

She threw a look upwards, her blue eyes wide with shock and alarm, and he laughed in angry mockery.

'Obviously you can't wait...'

What on earth was he talking about? Luisa tried to break free and his fingers tightened. He jerked her towards him until their bodies collided. She gave a little gasp, and began to tremble at the contact, then Zachary West's mouth came down hard against hers and the world went out of focus for an endless moment.

She didn't close her eyes; they remained open, dazed and incredulous, while her whole body reacted wildly to the touch of his mouth. She had never been so conscious of herself as a physical being. In that moment she really discovered her body for the first time, became aware of everything happening to it: her heart thudding inside her ribcage, her pulses going wild at throat, wrists, behind the ears, her blood racing in her veins, her lungs drawing air, her skin perspiring, her nostrils desperately sucking in air as if she were drowning, the heat and moisture between her thighs.

It had never happened to her before. She couldn't believe it was happening now.

One kiss and she wanted him desperately, with a desire that was like dying.

CHAPTER FOUR

IT HAD been a bad day for Zachary West. He had been awake half the night. He usually was. He was often afraid to go to sleep in case he had a nightmare. He had relived the accident hundreds of times since it happened. The shock of seeing the other car coming, the swerve as he pulled on his wheel, the crash and then the flames leaping up towards him.

To get his mind off the bad memories he had deliberately invoked another one and lay in bed thinking of the girl he had seen just before the crash, the girl in white who had floated through a garden in the dusk like a sweet dream. He had never forgotten her. During all these months of illness the memory of her had been something he could turn to in his darkest hours. He wished he could find her, but since the accident he had been terrified of driving a car. If he had to go out he rang for a taxi.

When he was strong enough to face it he would start searching for her. Somehow he knew that one day he would find her; he had a strangely certain belief that she was somewhere waiting for him.

He had got up that morning while it was still dark, made himself coffee and eaten a slice of toast, standing by the window watching a red sun rise out of the sea, listening to the sad cry of the gulls.

Later he had gone to his studio, which was icy cold because he had forgotten to turn on the central heating, and looked at the new canvas he had put up on his easel the day he last came home from hospital.

There was not a brush stroke on it. He hadn't painted since the accident.

But he made himself go through with this charade, the pretence of believing that he would paint, today, that everything was normal, that his life was getting together again.

Turning away from the bare canvas, he began to mix his palette, taking his time to choose colours, his movements slow, deliberate.

He picked up his sketch-pads and flicked through them, as if looking for a sketch of a landscape to transfer to the canvas. Some were old sketches, some finished, full of detail: a storm at sea, gulls on a ploughed field, bare trees with the sun rising behind them.

Others were just a few lines, hastily scratched in a moment and abandoned. He didn't see anything he wanted to paint. He never did.

Frustrated, angry, he picked up a brush, loaded it with red paint, and furiously attacked the bare canvas until you couldn't see any white.

Throwing down his brush, breathing hard, he walked unsteadily to the window and opened it, breathing in the cold December air, watching his breath turn into mist in front of him.

A robin sat on a bush, watching him. Zachary watched it back. Once he would have picked up a pad, sketched it. Now he just stared, then turned away. He didn't look at the formless red blur of the canvas, just went into the kitchen and made himself another cup of coffee. While he was drinking it the phone rang.

He answered reluctantly, tempted to ignore it. 'Yes?'

'Zachary, are you coming next week or not?'

He recognised the peremptory voice without needing to be told that the speaker was his sister, Flora, who lived in Provence with her French husband, Yves, a man, Zachary had always felt, of infinite patience and good humour, or he would never have put up with bossy Flora for ten years.

'I told you——' Zachary began, but Flora didn't let him finish; she rarely did. The five years which made her his older sister also, in her eyes, made her his superior and entitled to interrupt, lecture and browbeat as and when she chose.

'You can't stay there for Christmas! It must be freezing in that cottage. I don't suppose you've got much food in the place, the shops will all be shut over the holiday, and you ought to be with your family at Christmas. What's Christmas without children?'

'Peaceful!' he growled.

Flora was not amused. 'I'll book your ticket to Marseille; you can pick it up at Heathrow when you get there. You had better come on the twenty-third; you want to be here on Christmas Eve.'

'I don't,' he said doggedly. 'I am not coming, Flora. Don't waste your money on a ticket I shan't use.'

'Now, listen, Zac——'

'No, Flora!' he bit out, his voice vibrating with anger. 'I am not coming.'

The sound of his angry voice silenced her for a moment, and he less angrily said, 'Look, I appreciate the kind thought, but I wouldn't be good company. I'm in no mood to be a jolly uncle to Sammi and Claude—I would spoil your Christmas and I don't want to do that. So have a good time. My best wishes to Yves and his family, and to the kids, and I'll see you——'

'Dana will be staying with her parents,' Flora hurriedly said, sensing that he was about to ring off. 'I told her you were coming. She's dying to see you again, even though you were so horrible to her when she tried to see you in the hospital. She's a sweet-natured girl; she says she understands why you couldn't bear to let her see you then and she's ready to give you another chance, so you can't make me look stupid by not turning up!'

'Just watch me!' he had snarled. 'Flora, stop interfering in my life. Just leave me alone, will you?' Then he had slammed the phone down, taken his coffee, and gone back to his studio to brood and scowl at the thick red blotches he had scrawled on his canvas. It perfectly expressed his mood.

Flora kept trying to get him and Dana together again. Zachary wished his sister would stop interfering in his life, but she had been doing it for so long that she probably didn't stop to think what he wanted. She thought she knew what was best for him, and at the moment that included Dana. Flora couldn't understand why he had ever broken with Dana.

A ravishing blonde, Dana was a singer—a good one, he had to admit. She earned a lot of money, and Flora, who was practically minded, approved of that.

'Why have you split up with her?' she kept asking, but Zachary never answered. On principle he never told his sister anything. It saved time and gave Flora something to do, a little detective work which kept her occupied.

The truth was that, when Dana had had her affair with someone else, and Zachary had found out, they had had a furious row, he had told her that he never wanted to see her again—and he had meant it.

Flora had taken it upon herself to interfere, however. After he had had his first plastic surgery, and looked a little more human, she had rung Dana, who was singing at a London night-club, and Dana had visited him.

She had tried not to flinch when she first saw him, but Zachary had read the shock and distaste in her eyes even while she tried to smile.

'How are you, you poor darling?' she had cooed. 'I'd have been before, but Flora said you weren't well enough to see anyone. As soon as she rang and said it was OK to come I rushed over.'

He had stared at her as she babbled on and on, trying to cover up her dismay and only making it more obvious.

'What a cosy little room. You're looking great, absolutely great, darling. How soon will you come home, do you think?'

'No idea,' he had muttered, scowling. 'You had better go, Dana. Flora shouldn't have told you to come. I don't want any visitors.'

Autumn sunlight had given her hair a golden halo, gilded her fair skin, made her green eyes cat-bright. She was wearing the simplest of clothes which he knew from his experience of her had undoubtedly cost a fortune—a blue silk shift with tiny sleeves, a scooped neckline and a short skirt which left her long, tanned legs bare.

Her beauty didn't move him any more, though. He had discovered the real woman inside that lovely shell, and he was indifferent to her.

She ignored his curtness for a while, perched on the end of his bed, giving him a flirtatious smile, her green eyes veiled by a sweep of darkened lashes.

'Darling, aren't you the teeniest bit pleased to see me? Don't I even get a kiss?'

And she leaned down, her body stiff, closing her eyes, as if that was the only way she could bear to touch him.

He had turned white with rage. 'Are you deaf?' he had yelled. 'Get out of here! Get out, damn you! Get out!'

The door had opened and a flustered nurse had rushed in. 'Mr West, they can hear you all over the hospital! Please stop shouting!'

'Get her out of here!' he had snarled, and Dana had slid off his bed, her golden hair tossing back, and rushed away, pretending to be broken-hearted. As the door slammed behind her Zachary had begun to laugh wildly. Deciding he was on the verge of a nervous breakdown, the nurse had called his doctor.

'Don't worry, Doctor,' Zachary had reassured him when he arrived. 'I'm fine. I just had a visitor who couldn't quite bring herself to kiss the toad in case he didn't turn back into a prince.'

He could make jokes about it, but Dana's reaction had sunk deep into his soul. She had made him realise what he really looked like. The only women he had seen since the accident, apart from Flora and other relatives, had been nurses, trained not to show their reactions to injuries like his. Dana had shown him how most women were likely to feel about the way he looked.

Maybe that was another reason why he hadn't gone looking for his girl in white—he was afraid that when he did she would be appalled by his scarred face.

To stop himself thinking about that, after his sister's phone call, he had put on a sweater and an old jacket and gone out into the garden to chop logs.

A few minutes later, he had heard a car. He rarely had visitors. Startled and not too pleased by the interruption, he had walked round to the front of the cottage and seen a woman standing near the gate.

For a second he had an odd feeling of familiarity, but on closer inspection he couldn't remember ever seeing her before. She was rather pale, a slender woman with a fine-drawn face, emphasised by the way she wore her hair pulled back tightly and pinned into a chignon.

The last time a stranger had come to the cottage it had been some journalist looking for a story. Zachary had sent him away, assuring him that he would break his neck if the man came back.

'Can I quote you, Mr West?' the reporter had called from the safety of his car. They thought they were so funny! Zachary had never had much time for the Press.

Was this another journalist? he had wondered, scowling at the woman by the gate. 'Who are *you*?' he grated. 'What do you want?' He hadn't even tried to disguise his irritation and hostility.

When she said that she was a nurse, from Whinbury Hospital, he realised suddenly that he did remember her, though it was so many months since his short stay there.

He hadn't liked her. She had been a cold, starchy sort of female. She crackled when she walked along the ward in her immaculate white apron and cap. He bet she even starched her undies. She was the type of woman he disliked most. Bossy, like his sister, busy, organising. Even worse, she would keep talking to him a voice pitched to soothe and placate as if he were a fretful child, her eyes full of pity.

Zachary wouldn't stand for that. He wouldn't have people feeling sorry for him. He preferred to insult them. At least it stopped them in their tracks.

So he had pretended to believe that she had come to see him because she found him so attractive and hadn't been able to stay away.

That had given him a bitter sort of fun. Because, of course, attraction was the last thing she felt. He had known that from the way she looked at him, her eyes wide and dark with an emotion that could only be dismay. No doubt she had imagined that, by now, after several very expensive operations, his face would be almost normal—but Zachary knew it wasn't, yet. The plastic surgeon had warned him that he would need to go back for several other operations before he looked more or less as he once had.

So he had mocked her, made a grab for her and kissed her, only to have the woman sag at the knees, fainting with shock and horror, no doubt.

Zachary caught her before she hit the path and carried her into the house, pushed her down on to a couch in his sitting-room, forced her head between her knees, and went to get her a glass of brandy.

When he turned back she had sat up, and now she was scarlet with embarrassment.

'I'm so sorry, what must you think of me? I don't know what came over me——'

'I shouldn't have kissed you,' he said curtly, pushing the brandy into her hand.

'Oh, no, thank you,' she said, looking at it as if it might be poison.

He took her wrist and forced her to lift the glass to her mouth. 'Drink it and don't be tiresome.'

She took a swallow reluctantly, shuddered, and Zachary let go of her. He pulled a chair up beside the couch and sat down on it, facing her.

'Now, what do you want, Sister . . . ?'

'Gilbey,' she said, nursing the glass. 'I'm . . . my father is Harry Gilbey, you see.' She paused, staring at him as if expecting him to recognise her father's name. Zachary blankly stared back.

'Have I met him? I'm sorry, but——'

'He was in the other car,' she whispered, and for a second he wasn't sure what she meant. He stared at her, frowning.

'The other car?'

Her eyes steadily met his as it began to dawn on him. She nodded.

Hoarsely he said, 'He... it was him... the other driver?'

She nodded again, her face pale now.

Zachary swore.

She flinched. 'It wasn't like him, Mr West. He wasn't drunk, and he isn't usually a reckless driver; he... he'd been under a tremendous strain and... I'm not trying to make excuses for him, but——'

'That's what it sounds like! If you aren't making excuses, what are you doing?' Zachary said angrily and saw her bite her lower lip. She had a wide mouth, he noticed, the lower lip full and warm, contradicting the austere hairstyle and the buttoned-up manner.

'I only wanted to explain,' she whispered. 'To make you see why it happened.'

His brows met in a scowl. 'Were you in the car with him?'

She shook her head. 'I wish I had been; it would never have happened.'

'He was right over my side of the road, coming round a bend at a crazy speed; I didn't have a chance in hell of avoiding him—did he tell you that?'

'Yes, of course he told me. He takes all the blame, and he bitterly regrets what happened, believe me!'

Zachary laughed. 'Big of him. Was he injured?'

'A little...'

'What does that mean exactly?'

'Bruises and shock,' she whispered, watching the cynical curl of his mouth.

'And how long was he in hospital?'

With obvious reluctance she admitted, 'Just a night.'

Zachary smiled bitterly. 'I've been in and out of hospitals ever since.'

'I know,' she said, her blue eyes meeting his unflinchingly. 'And I'm very sorry about what's happened to you, Mr West. So is my father. Please believe me; he knows what he did and it weighs very heavily on him.'

'Not as heavily as it weighs on me!' He got up, scowling. 'What are you doing here, anyway? What do you want?'

She got up too and put the brandy glass down on a nearby table. 'I came to plead with you... I know my father was to blame—he doesn't dispute that...but...Mr West, you will recover completely in time, believe me. I've had wide experience of cases like yours and, although it isn't a rapid process, you will be back to normal eventually.'

'My face will never be what you call normal again!' Zachary was so angry that he was icy cold, his face set and his hands curled at his sides, which was just as well as he might otherwise have hit her.

She had the decency to pause, frowning before she said in a slow, serious voice, 'You're wrong. I can understand why you think that, but you are wrong, Mr West. It will take another year or so, but plastic surgery can work wonders, especially if you are in the hands of a top specialist, and I know you are. He's a wonderful surgeon; his reputation is the highest in the country.'

'And even he doesn't pretend that he can give me back my face the way it was!' Zachary laughed suddenly, remembering Dana. 'You should have seen my last girlfriend's face when she saw me after I'd had the latest surgery! I thought she was going to faint.'

Sister Gilbey flinched, paling even more, staring steadily at him. 'I'm sure she was just very worried for you, and very upset. I don't deny it's a slow business, but I assure you that in time they will give you back your face.'

'Don't lie to me!' he snapped. 'I know what I see in the mirror. I'm as ugly as hell now, and the chances are I always will be. No woman is going to swoon when she sees me, except with horror, the way you did.'

The colour ran up her face and she looked away. 'I didn't——'

'You did. You flaked right out when I kissed you. I had to carry you in here.'

'That wasn't why——' she began, her skin hot, and Zachary laughed angrily.

'Yes, don't bother to pretend. I know why you fainted.'

Her lashes fluttered against her cheek and she stopped protesting, her face full of conflicting emotion. He watched her with bitter amusement.

At last, he said curtly, 'Oh, I'm not blaming you for that. I see myself in the mirror every day. I can understand why it made you sick when I touched you.'

'No!' she broke out, her eyes lifting then, full of a distress he had no difficulty reading and could not doubt to be sincere. 'Please believe me; that wasn't how I felt, at all.'

Zachary was tired of talking about it. These days he preferred to forget his accident; he was trying hard to get back to ordinary life.

'OK, let's forget it, shall we?' he impatiently grated. 'Let's get back to the reason for your being here—what is it you want from me, Sister Gilbey?'

'I'm not sure if . . .' she stammered, and sighed. 'Have your lawyers told you . . . did you know . . . ?'

'For heaven's sake spit it out!' Zachary grated.

She did, huskily. 'My father had forgotten to renew his insurance.'

He stared at her. He had been in hospital so much that he had left all the details of the legal proceedings which sprang from the accident to his lawyers, refusing to discuss the matter with them other than to give them his own version of events, so he had never been told that Harry Gilbey had no insurance.

'You're kidding!' he said incredulously.

She shook her head, but was dumb, as if she couldn't bear to say another word.

Zachary stared into her eyes. They were an incredibly deep blue. He didn't think he had ever seen eyes quite that dark a blue before. Gentians in the winter snow of the Alps, that was what they reminded him of, their deep colour emphasised by the pallor of her face. Dark blue on white... He had always loved the contrast.

Then, more practically, he thought, no wonder she's pale, no wonder she's worried, no wonder she's here, pleading with me! What sort of man was this father of hers? Why had he sent her here to plead for him, instead of coming himself, or getting a lawyer to do it?

'How on earth could he be so irresponsible?' he said aloud, more to himself than her.

She swallowed, her long pale throat moving convulsively. 'He was under a terrible strain; he still is... in financial difficulties and unable to see a way out. That's why he forgot. He meant to renew his insurance when it lapsed, but... I know it was stupid, but——'

'Stupid doesn't cover it!'

'I'm not asking you to let him off——'

'Good,' he snapped. 'Because I wouldn't. Why the hell should I?'

She turned away, her head hanging, then turned back, those blue eyes lifted to him again, glistening with what he saw were unshed tears.

'His life will be ruined if he has to pay at once... He has a mortgage on his house, another on his business... There's no money in the bank; he would have to sell his home, maybe his firm, too, if he has to pay you a huge amount in damages.'

'None of this is my problem; it's his!' Zachary tersely told her. 'Just as the accident was his fault, all the consequences that flow from it are, too.' He gave her a stare, his mouth twisting in sardonic disbelief. 'You must be very naïve or very optimistic if you came here hoping that I'd waive my right to damages just because you gave me a sob story about your father's life being ruined!'

'I just thought that——' she began, and he cut her off, his voice curt.

'The only life that interests me is my own, and your father wrecked it last spring.'

Anguished, she cried, 'I know you were badly hurt, but you will recover. In a year's time you'll be back to normal!'

'I'll have lost several years of my life by then! That accident destroyed the work I had spent years on, I've been in pain ever since, and it isn't over yet by a long way. I can't even work any more. I haven't painted since the accident. I've been banging my head on a stone wall every day I've been here, trying to paint, but the impulse seems to have died in that crash. Every time I pick up the brush my hand and brain seem unconnected... Have you any conception how that feels? Not to be able to paint for me is like being paralysed. I might as well be dead!'

She listened, as if turned to stone, and Zachary looked down at her with eyes that burned with anger. All this resentment and rage had been boiling inside him ever since the accident. It was a strange relief to be able to let it all out.

This girl wasn't responsible for what had happened to him, but her father was, and she seemed to feel her father had suffered in the accident, too. That made Zachary so mad he could spit teeth.

'Don't ask me to feel sorry for your father!' he threw at her fiercely. 'If I were a saint, I might manage it—but I don't pretend to be a saint. When the case comes to court the damages will be decided on by other people, judging by the evidence. Your father will have to abide by their decision.'

'But if you would only——' she persisted, and Zachary's temper flared again.

'You didn't really believe you could talk me into dropping any claim for damages?' he mocked harshly, then his eyes narrowed, glittering with sudden cynicism as another line of thought occurred to him. 'Or haven't I got it right? Did you come to offer me something instead of the money?'

She looked back as if not understanding him, a bewildered look in her blue eyes.

Zachary began to laugh, deliberately letting his eyes wander down over her small, high breasts under the white sweater she wore, the soft curve of her hips and slim legs in smooth-fitting black trousers, and his stare was openly sensual and assessing.

She caught on at last and blushed. He heard the intake of her breath, and gave her a mocking little smile.

'Sorry,' he drawled, 'but you aren't my type. I rather like blonde girls with good bodies. You are much too skinny and I suspect you haven't had much experience and wouldn't be inventive enough in bed.'

She was crimson by then. If looks could kill, he would have been lying dead at her feet at that moment, Zachary thought with a sort of angry triumph, and then he suddenly wondered why he had lost his temper enough to want to taunt her. It wasn't after all her fault that this had happened to him! His mouth twisted in disgust. What the hell have I come down to? There was no need to insult the girl just because her father had caused his accident.

No need. Except . . . except, perhaps, that he had felt a prickle of sexual interest while he was looking her over, he accused himself. That was it, wasn't it? It had been a lie that she wasn't his type. He didn't have a type, if he was honest. He liked women. Full stop. And this one very definitely could be his type. Except that she would probably rather die. She'd passed out when he kissed her. If she knew he had felt a stab of desire for her just now she would have started running and wouldn't stop until she was a long way off.

'I wasn't offering anything of the kind!' she spluttered, and he laughed bitterly.

'No?' As if she needed to tell him that!

'I only wanted to suggest a . . . well, an arrangement . . .'

'Between us?' he drawled. 'What sort of arrangement are you offering? Or am I supposed to use my imagination?' Again he slid an appraising glance over her, and those blue eyes threw sparks

of fire back at him. Oh, she didn't like any sort of
sexual jokiness, did she? Prim and proper little
madam. Was that why she had gone into nursing?
Did the nun-like uniform suit her in more ways than
one?

'No,' she said shortly, very flushed now. 'Between you and my father. I thought that if you al-
lowed him to pay you gradually over some years
he needn't lose his home or his firm.'

Her tension and anxiety was so painful that
Zachary felt a twinge of compassion for her and
said flatly, 'Don't worry, I'm sure the courts will
work out something along those lines.'

'Will they?' Her eyes had not been reassured.

He had added, even more kindly, 'You know,
they always take people's situations into account
when they fix damages, and they certainly wouldn't
insist that he sell his home.'

There was desperation in her voice by then.
'Maybe not, but you don't understand... He
already has huge debts; it would be hard for him
to pay a large sum to you on top of that, and...'
She broke off, looking away, a struggle in her face,
then jerkily went on, 'And if his wife discovers how
much money he owes, he's afraid she'll leave him.'

He was exasperated. 'It isn't my fault if he's in
debt!'

'No, but if you could only agree to wait a year
or so for any damages the court may fix there's a
good chance she wouldn't find out. He's sure the
profits from the business will have nearly doubled
in two years' time, and then he could pay you,
gradually.'

Cynically, Zachary said, 'And I'm supposed to wait?'

She gave him a distressed, uncertain glance. 'Will that be very difficult for you? Are you hard up, too?'

'I'm not starving in the street,' he curtly admitted. 'Tell me, am I right in guessing that your father's wife is not your mother?'

She nodded. 'My mother died some years ago.'

'When did your father remarry?'

'A couple of years later.'

His grey eyes held teasing amusement. 'And you don't love your stepmother?'

'We don't get on,' she agreed coldly.

He considered her with curiosity and faint hostility. That was the face he remembered from his brief stay in her hospital. He had woken up at night and seen that cool, pure oval beside his bed: the blue eyes remote, her hair pulled back tightly to give her the look of a nun in her white and dark blue uniform. He had disliked her on sight, but she had looked different today, in that vivid red coat and the white sweater that clung to her body and made her look very female and distinctly desirable.

Now she was withdrawn and icy, and Zachary felt his hackles rising.

'Why don't you like her?'

'She doesn't like me!' Her voice was sharply defensive and he smiled to himself.

'Ah, but which came first, her dislike—or yours?' He could imagine how less than welcoming she must have been to the interloper. Since her mother's death, no doubt she and her father had been very close, drawn together by shared grief, and she would have been shocked when her father got over his loss and found another woman. How could he? she must have asked herself, outraged. He was her father. He was supposed to pine eternally for her mother, not marry again in a few years.

'I would have tried to like her, if she hadn't made it clear from the start that I wasn't wanted around any more!' she retorted, face tight with anger. 'She didn't want people to see us together. They might have thought she was my sister. She's only a couple of years older than I am.'

His black brows shot up. 'Really? How old is your father, then?'

'Fifty. He and my mother were very young when they got married.'

And how old is your stepmother?'

'She'll be thirty on her next birthday.'

He nodded, watching her thoughtfully. 'So you're what ... twenty-eight ... ?'

'Twenty-seven.'

'You look younger.' That remark was surprised out of him. He had imagined she must be in her early twenties. 'It must be the virginal look,' he drily added, and she blushed again. He gave her a mocking smile. 'Virginal isn't a rude word, you know.'

'You make it sound like one.'

He laughed, his teasing eyes wandering down over her body, her breasts high under the clinging sweater, her waist slender, her hips and legs smoothly feminine.

'You're just too sensitive on the subject,' he drawled, then abruptly asked, 'Are you one?'

She jumped, gasping, as if a bee had stung her. 'What?'

'A virgin,' he gravely said, although he knew she had understood what he meant.

She stuttered, blushing furiously now. 'I...I...I'm not answering questions like that!'

'I had a feeling you were,' he said, hugely amused by her shocked confusion. 'Although it seemed very unlikely, at your age! I don't think I can remember meeting one for years, unless it was some kid in her teens. Virginity went out of fashion in the sixties; I wonder if it's coming back? Are you part of a trend? Or are you just weird?'

'If you're going to make stupid jokes I'm going...' she threatened, on her feet and poised for flight.

'Maybe it's one effect of the Aids crisis?' he thought aloud. 'Tell me more about your stepmother.'

She turned on her heel and began hurrying towards the door.

'You haven't had your answer yet,' Zachary called after her.

She looked back coldly. 'You've had your fun, Mr West. I'm not staying here to be a target for your idea of wit any longer.'

'The accident has warped my sense of humour a little.' He shrugged, not intending to apologise any further than that.

'I noticed,' she said, her pale mouth tight.

'But I am prepared to discuss making some sort of arrangement with your father to make sure he doesn't lose either his home, his business, or his wife,' he said, watching her intently.

She took a step towards him, her lips parting on a gasp and her face alight with eagerness.

'Really? You aren't making fun of me again?'

'I'm serious,' Zachary said. 'On certain conditions.'

She tensed, eyes wary again. 'What conditions?'

'That you move in here with me, for as long as I want you.'

CHAPTER FIVE

LUISA felt as if he had slapped her face. Her skin turned scalding hot, then she went white with temper.

'I should have known better than to listen!' she said angrily. 'Does it make you feel better to be so unpleasant to me, Mr West? I'm sorry for you. I wouldn't want to be in your shoes for a second, and not just because of all the pain you've had. What I find horrifying is the way it has warped your mind.'

She didn't wait for him to react; she turned on her heel and hurried out of the cottage. The early morning mist had cleared, and she could see for miles—fields on one side, the grey North sea on the other. As she unlocked her car, Zachary West emerged and stood in his doorway, the wind blowing his thick dark hair across his scarred face.

He brushed it back with one hand and called to her, 'My offer was serious. If you decide to take me up on it, let me know before the case comes to court. After that it will be too late.'

She ignored him, got into her car, and drove away. But she was so jittery after the encounter with Zachary West that she drove badly, and only just missed hitting another car at a junction just outside the village, and so she parked on the far side of Tareton, in a lay-by, and tried to calm down.

The things he had said kept coming back, making her wince. A virgin, he had deduced, and the most galling thing about that was that it was true. How had he known? Did it show in her face? She pulled down a flap which had a mirror behind it and stared at herself.

What was it that gave her away? Did experience leave behind visible traces which couldn't be found in her face?

She couldn't even say why she had never been to bed with anyone, either. There had been men she had wanted to make love with, but somehow it had never got that far. Maybe because she was living in the nurses' home, during her probationary years? That had made it difficult to go to bed with anyone who didn't have their own place, and most of her dates had been with young doctors who also lived in hospital quarters. Not that they hadn't all tried— in cars, in other people's flats, after parties . . . but Luisa had never been able to relax enough.

There was something so furtive and hurried about those encounters, and she had wanted her first time to be special, romantic, beautiful.

When she qualified she had moved out to live with her father again, to look after him, and that had been another, different barrier. She couldn't make love with anyone when her father was out in case he came back suddenly.

She gave an angry little groan, biting her teeth. Stop kidding yourself! she thought. The truth was she'd never wanted anyone enough to go to bed with them. She had been attracted now and then, liked someone well enough to enjoy their company, but there had never been a great passion, a blinding need which had demanded satisfaction.

Until half an hour ago she had never felt burning desire, hadn't known what it meant—until Zachary West kissed her, in fact.

She shivered, closing her eyes. She still hadn't got over that moment. It was hard to believe it had happened.

She had known he attracted her, of course. When she first met him, in the hospital, even when he looked far worse than he did now—she had known then.

It wasn't just physical. There was some sort of emotional tug, as if everything he did, every movement, every glance of his eyes, even the sound of his breathing was important to her.

Oh, stop it! she told herself irritably and started the car again. She wouldn't tell her father she had been to see Zachary West. He would be horrified if he knew. She was certain Zachary West wouldn't mention it to anyone, either.

Christmas Day was a good day to spend in the hospital. There was a wonderful atmosphere on every ward, even though some patients wept because they missed their homes. The children's ward was the most poignant, but oddly enough adults found that sadder than the children themselves, who were being so spoilt and showered with presents and attention, from their families and the staff, that most of them had a great time.

On Luisa's ward there were some very ill patients who didn't know it was Christmas at all. Her day was rather quieter than it was on other wards, but she and her staff had put up decorations and had a little Christmas tree glittering with silver bells and red velvet ribbons.

Her father had already delivered her Christmas present, a new dressing-gown, warm blue velvet, the day before he and Noelle flew to Switzerland. He and Luisa only had time for a drink together and an exchange of presents: he had to hurry back home to pack. Luisa had got him the latest thriller by his favourite writer and a skiing sweater which he had said he would like. They always had given each other broad hints about what presents to buy; that way they got what they really wanted.

On Boxing Day Luisa voluntarily put in a morning in Casualty, which was very short-staffed, but having a typical rush of people who had had accidents over the festive season. There was a man with a fishing-hook embedded in his palm, a woman who had cut the top of her finger almost to the bone, while slicing cold turkey, a little boy who had fallen off his new Christmas bicycle and broken a wrist, someone who had a bad sprain from taking part in a Boxing Day long-distance race, someone else who had a broken rib from playing rugby that morning.

'Thanks for helping out,' the young Casualty doctor said as they broke for a much-needed coffee during a brief lull in the rush.

'I've enjoyed it,' Luisa said and meant it. 'A change is as good as a holiday.'

'I'd rather have the holiday!' the other girl said wryly.

'Well, just between us, so would I!' Luisa laughed and the Indian girl did too, but her eyes darkened when Luisa added, 'And anyway, my family are away—they went to Switzerland for Christmas.'

'Mine, too,' Dr Kumar said, sighing. 'Although we don't celebrate Christmas, of course.'

'But they're in Switzerland?'

'No, in Delhi!' Indira Kumar said, and they both began giggling until a new arrival pushed through the Casualty doors. Indira put down her cup. 'Here we go again!'

Luisa got up more slowly, flushed and startled. What on earth was Zachary West doing here?

Indira walked away, her white coat flapping, and Luisa moved to intercept Zachary West, her eyes hostile.

'What are you doing here?'

He met her stare drily. 'Well, I wasn't looking for you, so you can stop getting agitated!' he drawled and held out his hand.

Only then did she see the deep cut just below his thumb. It had stopped bleeding. But it looked painful.

'How did you do that?' she asked, taking his hand and inspecting the wound more closely. It had clean edges and had laid his hand open as if it had been sliced by a knife so she wasn't surprised when he said,

'Chopping wood. The axe slipped.'

'You really should be more careful,' she scolded.

'Yes, Nanny.'

She looked up at the dry mockery, her face serious. 'The last thing you need is any more injuries. It could lead to nasty complications. When did you last have a tetanus shot?'

'No idea. Years ago, I expect.'

'Well, you had better see Dr Kumar, then I'll give you a tetanus shot and clean your wound before it's stitched up.'

'Yes, Nanny,' he said in the same tone, his face mocking, and her mouth tightened as she steered him towards Indira's office.

He was determined to make fun of her, but she wasn't going to let him annoy her. She was going to keep her cool.

She knocked on Indira's door. 'Come in,' Indira promptly said and Luisa showed Zachary into the little room. As she had expected, she was told to give him a tetanus shot and clean his wound then bring him back to have it stitched. If they had been very busy, Luisa could have done the stitching herself, but, as it was, at the moment Indira had nothing to do but catch up with her paperwork, which she was always glad to escape from. Paperwork was one of the curses of the modern medical profession, thought Luisa, ushering Zachary out of the office again.

He grimaced as she prepared the tetanus shot. 'I hate injections.'

'Everybody does,' she said without sympathy.

'They haven't all had as many as I've had,' he growled.

He was brave, she thought, watching him secretly from behind her lashes as she gave him the tetanus injection and then a local anaesthetic directly into the area of the wound. He closed his eyes, briefly;

she saw his jaw clench and heard an intake of breath, but he didn't make another sound, only sighed once she had finished.

Straightening, Luisa had a passionate impulse to comfort him, stroke his black hair, put her arms around him as if he were a child, but of course she didn't dare. She could imagine his expression, what he would say.

His voice steady, he asked her, 'When did you move to this ward?'

'I didn't—I'm only here for today. Christmas upsets all the rotas. The usual sister on this ward has children. She badly wanted to spend Christmas with them, but she's short-staffed—we all are. So to help out I offered to take over for today.'

'Did you have Christmas Day off?'

She shook her head. 'Come along, we had better go back to Dr Kumar now, to get that wound stitched.'

He fell into step beside her. 'You worked yesterday and you're voluntarily working today? What about your family? What do they think of that?'

'My father and stepmother are in Switzerland, skiing.'

'So you had nowhere to go for Christmas, anyway?'

She felt him watching her and fought to keep her face blank and her voice calm. 'That's right.' She knocked on Indira's door and stood back to let him pass her, grateful that he couldn't go on asking these personal questions now.

He watched stoically as Indira put neat stitches into the wound, her small hands deft and accustomed.

'You must be very good at embroidery,' he said, and Indira looked up and grinned at him.

'I am—my mother taught me to sew as soon as I was old enough to hold a needle. She wanted me to become a dressmaker.'

'How did she react when you said you wanted to be a doctor?'

'Oh, my mother is old-fashioned; she doesn't think girls need an education.' Indira shrugged.

'She wanted you to get married?'

Indira nodded. 'My mother would sell her teeth to get a better future for her sons, but she thinks it is wasting money to educate girls, and, anyway, she was afraid I would get western ideas about equality and maybe even marry someone my family did not like.'

'So how did you manage to become a doctor in the end?'

'Luckily, my father had always wanted to be a doctor. He said I should to go medical school if I qualified for it, and I worked like a donkey to make sure I did, of course.'

'And your mother accepted it?'

Indira smiled her secretive little smile. 'My mother always accepts it when my father makes a decision. Not that she doesn't try to persuade him to do something else at first, but once he has said, "This will happen!" then she stops arguing and accepts it. She says this is the secret of a happy marriage, and, for my father, it is, of course.'

'Is that *your* idea of a happy marriage?'

'I think decisions should be taken together, and a compromise be reached which both accept,' Indira said. 'But I am glad my father is happy; he is a wonderful man and I owe him a great deal.'

'He must be very proud of you,' said Zachary West, smiling at her as she finished off her work on his hand. 'That is a first-rate job you've done on me, and I am an expert, believe me. I have been operated on by some of the top surgeons in London!'

Indira laughed. 'Well, thank you, I shall treasure the compliment! And yes, my father is delighted that I am a qualified doctor, working in a hospital. I'm his dream come true, I suppose.' Her black eyes twinkled. 'Actually, when I first began to work here he kept popping in just to look at me and tell people I was his daughter!'

'That's nice,' Zachary said. 'I shall be tempted to pop in myself and tell them you sewed up my hand!'

Indira blushed and giggled again. 'You must not flirt with me, Mr West. I am engaged to be married to a very jealous surgeon in this hospital. He would not like it if he heard you.'

'Does your father approve of him, too?'

'Very much—his family come from Delhi, like mine.' Catching Zachary's eye, she laughed and shook her head. 'No, it wasn't an arranged marriage, but both our families are pleased. In fact, at the moment my parents are visiting his home to discuss the wedding arrangements.'

Luisa listened in surprise and a faint chagrin. She had known Indira for months, since Casualty was often the arrival point for many of the patients who ended up in Luisa's burns unit, but she had never got her talking so freely about herself, her family and background. Why was it that Zachary West, who was always so offhand with her, got on so well with Indira?

Of course Luisa knew about Indira's engagement, since her fiancé, Girish, had been working with the ear, nose and throat team for several years. He was an attractive man, with liquid dark eyes, smooth olive skin and a charming smile, very well liked in the hospital.

Zachary got up to leave and Indira told him firmly, 'Don't use that hand too much for a few days. We don't want those stitches bursting.'

'I'll be careful, Doctor,' he promised.

Luisa followed him out. 'I must make an appointment for you to come and have those stitches taken out, Mr West.'

Consulting the appointments book, she suggested a date and time and he nodded. 'OK.' She wrote out a card for him and he pocketed it, studying her with narrowed eyes.

'So you're working all over Christmas? Don't you mind that?'

She shook her head, watching the receptionist dealing with a newcomer with a small child. Just as Luisa was on the point of going over there the woman walked off along the corridor towards the X-ray department, and Luisa turned back to answer Zachary West. 'I'm used to it. Obviously married staff with children get priority at these times, and, anyway, Christmas can be very special in a hospital. Lots of the staff want to work because they enjoy it so much, especially those who live alone.'

'Like you,' he drily said.

Luisa didn't bother to answer that.

'And like me,' he added, and she gave him a quick look.

'Haven't you got a family you could go to?'

'My sister invited me, but you need to be fit to survive a few days with her kids—they're domestic terrorists. They wreck everything they touch, and need to be entertained all the time. They won't go out and play in the garden, or go for walks—even the beach is boring to them. No, if it isn't constant TV or videos it's those damned electronic games or noisy rock music. Life in that household is hell when they're home from school.'

'Where do they live?'

'Provence.'

She was startled, having expected him to say London or somewhere near by.

'In France?'

'When I last looked at a map,' he sardonically agreed.

'Lucky them,' she said, her dark blue eyes dreamy as she imagined it. 'However noisy your sister's children, I'd have gone like a shot. I wish someone would offer me a trip to Provence.'

'OK, then, I'll go if you will,' he said, taking her breath away.

After giving him a stunned, incredulous look she decided to treat it as a joke and laughed.

'Very funny.'

'I wasn't joking.'

Confused and irritated, Luisa turned away. 'I'm sorry, Mr West; I don't have time to play one of your games. I'm needed to deal with patients.'

The ward was getting busier again. Several new patients had arrived and were being processed by the receptionist and a younger nurse, who asked them to sit down and wait to be seen either by Dr Kumar or herself.

Whinbury was not a big hospital, or a busy one most of the time. The town was quite small, the area very rural. Their casualty department was no-where near as busy as that of a big town hospital. In this hospital a patient could be in and out within half an hour, at most an hour or so. There was little hope of such a fast turnaround in London, Luisa knew, and was grateful that she worked in such a tranquil little backwater, although she meant one day to take a job in London for a year or two, just for the experience.

As she walked over to the reception desk she heard Zachary West's footsteps echoing as he strode to the exit across the stone-tiled floor, and then heard him ask the porter to get him a taxi.

Of course, she thought, he couldn't drive with that injured hand, even as she was briskly asking, 'What have we got now?' as her junior nurse handed her a little pile of neatly filled-out cards.

Luisa glanced through them, aware of Zachary hovering near the main door. Concentrate! she told herself crossly. Forget him. Keep your mind on the job. But although she never looked his way again she knew when his taxi arrived and he left, and her body slackened in a mixture of relief and regret as he went.

She was feeling like death by the time she left. Indira Kumar asked, 'So how was your day in Casualty?' and she groaned.

'I'd forgotten just how tiring it is. I was on my feet nearly all day, and I'm shattered.'

Indira grinned. 'You've been having a restful time in the Burns Unit, obviously.'

'I sit down a lot more, anyway!'

'We never get time to sit down for long. That's the nature of the job. But you were brilliant, Luisa. I could do with you here full-time.' Indira gave her a coaxing smile. 'If you ever want to come back, I'd welcome you with open arms. And you would soon get used to it again. Think of all the weight you'd lose, too.'

Luisa laughed, but shook her head. 'Sorry, Indira. I like it where I am. The work is hard, but it is worthwhile. I feel I'm doing something really valuable there.'

Indira sobered, sighing. 'Yes, of course. I understand. Pity. Well, enjoy your days off. Will you be seeing David?'

'No, he's gone to Wales to have Christmas with his parents.'

'He didn't ask you to go with him?' Indira caught her glance and grimaced. 'Sorry, was that a tactless question? I just thought...you and David have been going out for months now; I imagined it was...well, serious. Or serious enough for him to want you to spend Christmas with him, anyway.'

'Not yet,' Luisa said, a little flushed. David had, in fact, suggested that she spend Christmas in Wales with his family, but at the time she had expected to be spending the holiday with her own family, and when her father broke it to her that he and Noelle were going to Switzerland Luisa hadn't told David in case he repeated his own invitation. She didn't want to go away with him, meet his family, allow herself to be drawn into a deeper commitment.

She still saw him quite often, but their relationship hadn't really progressed during the last few months. They had both been busy—work took up most of their lives—but she knew that David was getting impatient with her, that he wanted their relationship to become more intimate. They had been dating for months; he was pressing her to sleep with him. She knew he was frustrated and upset over her refusal, and hated hurting his feelings, but she still wasn't going to sleep with him just to make him feel better about himself. She wasn't a consolation prize for a man with an ego problem.

That evening, while she was making herself a stir-fried dinner of turkey and seasonal vegetables in her wok, she kept thinking over her day, remembering the way her heart had turned over sickeningly when she saw Zachary West.

He was the first man she had ever wanted this way. Only now did she understand how David felt when he had her in his arms: maybe passion was always one-way? David wouldn't think it was funny if she was ever tactless enough to tell him that Zachary West could light her fire merely by looking at her, whereas David had never managed it, hard as he tried.

She bit her lip, turning her hot food out on to a plate. Zachary West had been amusing himself with her, and she knew it, even while she was burning up with fever when he kissed her. She must stop thinking about him!

Next day was clear and bright, although it was cold, and Luisa was restless so she went out for a drive mid-morning. She took the road out of Whinbury which led towards the sea, vaguely telling herself that she might find somewhere nice to have lunch along the coast. She knew several pleasant seaside hotels which did light lunches.

The village of Tareton was as silent as the grave when she drove through it. The roads were quite empty, too. Most people were still recovering from Christmas, or, if they did go out driving, were going to the nearest town to do some shopping at the winter sales which always started immediately after Christmas.

By the time Luisa was in sight of Zachary West's cottage she had admitted to herself that she had always known she would end up there.

She even had an excuse ready to offer him, but when he opened his front door and confronted her the words dried up on her tongue.

His brows arched in dry amusement. 'Hello, again. Changed your mind about that trip to Provence?'

CHAPTER SIX

LUISA was furious to feel herself redden. Why did she have to keep blushing every time she saw him? No wonder he kept making fun of her!

'Actually, I came to check that you had some sort of help in the house so that you won't be tempted to use your injured hand.'

He eyed her sardonically. 'Are you a social worker as well as a nurse?'

'Of course not, but as I happened to be driving this way...' Her voice trailed off as she looked over his shoulder into the cottage and caught sight of a scene of confusion and turmoil: books scattered all over the floor, drawers pulled out of a sideboard, tumbled objects everywhere. 'Good heavens...' she muttered, horrified. 'What on earth have you been doing? You aren't moving, are you?' The cottage had been tidy enough when she visited him before Christmas, but he was an artist, after all. Maybe he liked living in the midst of chaos?

'No,' he grimly told her. 'When I got back from the hospital yesterday, I found I'd been burgled.'

'Burgled?' she repeated, her blue eyes widening. 'Oh, no! That's terrible. Was anything valuable taken?'

'My TV, my video machine, my stereo equipment and my microwave oven. In other words, anything they could sell easily.'

'Have the police been?'

'They only came half an hour ago, and they didn't stay long. They told me they were short-staffed because it was Christmas and my house wasn't the only one that had been burgled during the holiday. They said they were run off their feet answering calls. They didn't find any fingerprints, or any clues, as far as I know, and I didn't get the impression they expected to catch anyone, let alone get my stuff back.'

Luisa stared past him at the sitting-room. 'Have you got a cleaner who will come in and tidy up for you?'

'I've got a cleaner who has the week off for Christmas, which she is spending in a hotel in Harrogate, so she won't be tidying up for me. I was just about to start work on the mess when you arrived.'

'I'll give you a hand,' Luisa said on impulse. If she had expected him to protest or argue she was disappointed.

'I hoped you'd offer,' he said, coolly, and stepped back. 'And if we finish in time I'll buy you a pub lunch from the Black Swan in Tareton. Best pub lunches for miles. But you'll have to drive us there because I can't drive at the moment, as you'll recall.'

Luisa took off her cherry-red jacket. 'If you have food in the house I can always make us a snack meal later, anyway. Now, is this the only room they vandalised?'

'Yes. They obviously went upstairs, but it was the stuff down here they wanted and they probably wanted to get away with it before I came back so they didn't waste too much time smashing the place up. The police tell me I got away lightly. They had seen much worse damage.'

'Not much comfort,' Luisa said, and he grimaced.

'No.'

It was not an easy job and Luisa had been rather weary to start with, after working hard for days, but she was used to hard work and had a dogged instinct to finish whatever she started, so she kept going until the cottage had been restored to normal. She was not so tired that, some time later, she didn't notice Zachary's pallor, and ordered him to sit down and rest and leave the job to her.

'I'm fine,' he said shortly.

'No, you're not. Sit down and don't be obstinate. What good will it do for you to make yourself ill again?'

He considered her, his mouth twisting. 'I don't like bossy women!'

'I didn't ask you to like me,' she retorted, but a painful little knife ground round and round inside her as he said it. 'I only want you to use your common sense and sit down before you fall down.'

'Oh, very well.' He shrugged and slowly made his way to a chair. Satisfied, Luisa got on with the work while he watched her for some time; then he went out to the kitchen. To her surprise, he came back with a pot of coffee and a plate of thickly cut sandwiches.

'The pub just shut so we won't be able to go there for lunch. I have a limited choice for sandwiches—cheese or salad. Which do you want?'

'Either will do for me,' she said, concentrating on what she was doing.

He gave her a dry look. 'Stop trying to get the scratches out of that table and go and wash, then we'll eat.'

She put a finger on one of the deeply scored marks left by the burglars, her face regretful. 'What on earth makes people do such mean and spiteful things? This table is ruined and it looks quite old.'

'It's late Georgian,' Zachary said, frowning so that his scarred face became the threatening mask which made people back away in shock. His voice was wryly resigned, though. 'Oh, not very valuable, but it has been in my family since 1820 so I wouldn't want to lose it. It can be put right, I hope. I know someone who renovates old furniture—he does wonders. I'll give him a ring.'

'Good.' Luisa glanced around the room. 'I think I've done everything,' she thought aloud.

'Yes, you have, so go and wash! The bathroom is upstairs on the landing, to the left.'

She ran upstairs and found the bathroom immediately. It was charming: lemon-yellow and full of light. She fingered one of the fluffy yellow towels, wondering if he had chosen the accessories in the room, which all matched. On the pinewood vanity unit she found a freshly unwrapped bar of lemon-scented soap laid out. Especially for her? Or was it just coincidence?

When she returned to the sitting-room Zachary had laid out coffee-cups and plates on the table by the french windows.

As she appeared he poured out the coffee, and suddenly Luisa realised how hungry she was—her nostrils quivered at the delicious fragrance and she swallowed.

'Sit down and eat,' Zachary said, placing half a cheese sandwich on a plate and pushing it over to her.

She gave the thick bread a glance, amused. 'Do you eat sandwiches for lunch often?'

'When I'm working, yes. I can't spare the time to cook or go off in search of lunch at the pub. I only go there when I'm not busy painting.'

'Do you work every day?' she asked, before biting into her sandwich, which she found had a huge chunk of Cheddar cheese inside it, spiced up with some sort of tomato chutney which had a home-made taste and feel to it.

There was a pause. She looked up and saw dark red in his face, his mouth tight. What was annoying him now? He was a very touchy man, but then he was having a bad time lately. The accident, the scars it had left, both mental and physical, and now a burglary—who wouldn't be irritable in his shoes?

'I used to,' he tersely muttered at last, and because she was ultra-sensitive where he was concerned she picked up something of the distress that lay behind the words and her heart ached for him.

'You still can't start working normally?'

He glared at her resentfully, glowering. 'I told you when you came to see me before—since the accident I haven't been able to paint. Oh, I'm not physically crippled. I could paint, if only I wanted to—it's the urge to do it that has withered. I can never make up my mind what I want to paint. I stand there for hours staring at the canvas and trying to decide, but...' He broke off, scowling, and she looked at him with sympathetic eyes.

'I'm sorry, it must be upsetting for you——'

'My God!' he roared, turning fierce silvery eyes on her. Luisa flinched, dropping her half-eaten sandwich back on to the plate. 'Of all the glib... Upsetting?' he repeated in scathing tones. 'Upsetting?' he shouted, baring his teeth at her. 'Woman, it is driving me out of my mind! I'm a painter. I need to paint and I don't understand why I can't; I keep trying and the more I try the worse it seems to get.'

She moistened her dry lips. Tentatively she murmured, 'Maybe you should stop trying and leave it for a week or so?'

'Do you think I haven't? I've tried everything I could think of, but nothing works.' He looked at her furiously. 'Oh, finish your sandwich! And drink that coffee before it gets cold.'

She obeyed meekly, in the hope of calming him down. It wasn't good for him to rage like this.

'Finished?' Zachary asked ten minutes later, as she drank her second cup of coffee.

'Yes, thank you, and the sandwiches were delicious.'

Zachary got to his feet. 'Come with me!'

Puzzled, she got up, too. 'Where?'

'My studio.'

He strode away and she followed, her curiosity aroused. She had never been in an artist's studio before and was dying to see what it was like.

His studio turned out to be an annexe to the cottage, at the back, two walls of it made up of sliding windows from ceiling to floor so that even on a dark winter day the room was full of light.

A canvas stood on an easel in the centre of the room. Zachary gestured to this with a peremptory hand. 'That is all the work I've done over the past nine months!'

She stared, baffled, at the angry red brush strokes covering the canvas.

'I don't know much about modern art, I'm afraid,' she politely said, and he glared.

'That isn't art, you stupid woman! I got so frustrated the other day that I just flung a lot of red paint at the canvas to express my feelings.'

Luisa unhappily murmured, 'I see... I'm s——'

'Don't say "sorry" again or I may hit you!' he roared.

She backed away nervously towards the glass wall on one side. 'What else can I say?'

The sun suddenly came out and lit her slender figure in the kingfisher-blue dress she was wearing. Zachary's eyes narrowed on her.

'Stand still,' he abruptly muttered.

'Why?' she asked in wary surprise, her dark blue eyes puzzled.

Zachary had picked up a sketch-pad and a piece of charcoal from a desk. She watched the long fingers of his uninjured hand move swiftly, black lines appearing on the white paper.

'Are you drawing me?' she asked, pleased, yet taken aback.

'What do you think I'm doing?'

She was too flattered to mind his growl. He had started work at last, and she had inspired him! A glow of pleasure went through her.

He flung down the charcoal after a moment and looked at the sketch, his mouth indented.

'Can I see?' asked Luisa, and he held out the pad without speaking. She stared, impressed by the few lines, the immediate resemblance to herself. 'That's wonderful! You're very talented, Mr West. I envy you—I don't have any artistic talent at all.'

'You're a very good nurse—that's no mean gift!' he said offhandedly.

Her colour rose. 'Thank you, but it isn't the same, is it? There are thousands of good nurses, but not so many artists. When will you transfer the sketch to canvas?'

'What?' He looked up, gave her a sarcastic smile. 'That isn't very likely, I'm afraid. I've always been able to sketch—that's a reflex action, just putting down what I see in front of me; it only takes a few minutes. A painting is very different—it needs many hours of work. It can take weeks, months... and first and foremost it needs inspiration, it needs me to know exactly what I'm looking for, and that's what has been missing all these months—the drive to create.'

She bit her lip. 'Oh. I see.' She felt a fool, humiliated. He probably thought her vain, and no doubt despised her for having imagined that she had inspired him.

He tossed the pad down and joined her by the window. 'What do you think of my garden? I designed it myself. Of course you aren't seeing it at its best—December is one of the deadest months in the year—but I planted a lot of evergreen shrubs—they give plenty of cover from the sea winds—and already you can see green shoots where the snowdrops, daffodils and crocuses are starting to show.'

She turned to stare out. 'You're a keen gardener?'

'I find gardening a soothing way of passing the time,' he agreed, then pointed. 'Look, there's my favourite magnolia—it will be covered in little white stars soon.'

She felt his shoulder touching hers, picked up the warm male scent of his body, and her heart began beating like a wild drum.

Gazing the way he pointed, she saw the small tree, leafless and yet covered in pale furry buds, but saw it through a haze, too aware of the man standing so close to her to concentrate on anything else.

Horrified by her own emotions, she turned hurriedly away just as Zachary moved. They collided; Luisa instinctively put out her hands to stop herself falling, her fingers latching into his cream wool sweater.

'Sorry...' she stammered, shooting a confused look upwards and praying that he couldn't read in her face her disturbing physical reaction to this contact with him.

The scarred face was tight with cynicism, the silvery eyes coldly mocking.

'You should be more careful,' he drawled. 'And don't tremble like that! I might misread your agitation as an invitation, remember. You hated it when I kissed you last time. In fact, you found it so repulsive that you fainted. You wouldn't want that to happen again, would you?'

She was appalled, both by what he said and how he said it. Did he really think he was so repulsive that she had fainted just because he kissed her?

'I didn't find you...' she began, then broke off, unsure how to phrase a denial without making it sound like an invitation. 'I mean... that wasn't why... Oh, don't think...' Her eyes were distressed and filled with compassion as she looked up at him. 'You mustn't think you aren't still very attractive...'

'No?' he mocked, laughing harshly. 'In that case...' And he slid his arms around her waist, moving a step closer so that their bodies touched. Her heart turned over as she felt the sensual movements of his hands, one holding her firmly at the waist while the other wandered, stroking slowly up her spine, urging her towards him, then sliding up to the nape of her neck, his cool fingers caressing.

Luisa began to tremble violently with a response she couldn't control. She felt as if she had been idly standing on a beach when without warning she was engulfed by a high tide, swept away, unable even to struggle, drowning in the wild rush of waves too powerful for her strength to fight.

She closed her eyes to shut out the world around them—the quiet room, the garden beyond the window, the everyday solidity of things which might have warned her about the folly of giving in to her feelings, brought her back from the erotic whirlpool into which he was pulling her. Her common sense might nag away, but Luisa didn't want to listen to it. For this one moment, anyway, she needed to experience the pleasures she had only dreamt about until now, and when his hard mouth touched the yielding warmth of her own she sighed with intense satisfaction and ran her arms around his neck, giving herself up to that kiss.

His hand pushed into the small of her back, propelling her even closer; his mouth grew hot and demanding, and she felt his body moving restlessly against her own. He wanted her. Her pulses went crazy and she felt fire leaping inside her.

But was it really her he wanted, or had he been without a woman for so long that any woman would have aroused him like this? a quiet little voice asked inside her head.

Angrily she refused to listen. What difference did it make why he wanted her, so long as he did?

The truth was that she had wanted him from the first moment she saw him, although for a long time she hadn't recognised her feelings for what they were, partly because it was the first time she had ever felt that way.

She had believed she was moved by his suffering, her heart wrung by the pain he was in at every waking moment. She had often been touched by patients in such pain; she had told herself her feelings for Zachary West were just the normal ones of a nurse for someone they were caring for, but this time compounded by her sense of guilt because she knew her father was responsible for his condition.

She had been lying to herself. Gradually she had been forced to recognise that. The intensity of her feelings was not due to pity for Zachary. The roots of those feelings were buried deep inside her own body; she wanted him, fiercely.

She had often wondered if she was frigid, incapable of the sort of love poets wrote about, love-song singers sang about.

Zachary West had proved to her that she wasn't.

His mouth left hers reluctantly, but he didn't lift his head. His lips slid down her cheek to her neck, lingeringly kissing behind her ear, and then the smooth skin of her throat, while one of his hands began to undo the round buttons on her kingfisher-blue dress.

Luisa's fingers pushed into his hair, and clenched on the thick vitality of the black strands which seemed to cling to her skin, curling around her fingers.

Zachary's lips crept from her throat downwards and she moaned with intense excitement. His face burrowed hotly into the valley between her soft, firm breasts; she felt him turn his head and then there was the strangest, most erotic sensation as she felt his lashes stir against one of her nipples.

A quiver ran through her. She could hardly breathe, but then Zachary's tongue caressed her breast and she couldn't stop herself giving a high, ecstatic cry.

As if the sound broke some spell which had held them both, Zachary stiffened, froze, unmoving. Then after a moment he lifted his head, breathing thickly, his scarred face dark red with heat.

She didn't want to come down to earth from the heaven he had taken her to, but she couldn't keep her eyes shut forever. Reluctantly, she opened them. The cold winter daylight seemed to dazzle her as, dazed and half blind with passion, her whole body shuddering, she risked a look up at Zachary.

His face was tense and pale now. He let go of her with an angry gesture and stepped back, away from her, his hands falling to his sides, still breathing as if he had been running in a life-or-death race.

'I'm sorry,' he muttered in a deep, husky voice. 'God, don't look at me like that! You're shivering like a rabbit in a trap.' He put a hand out as if to touch her, then let it drop again. 'It's OK, I've come to my senses. It won't happen again—you can stop shaking! I only meant to make a point—it started out as a stupid joke. I should never have laid a finger on you!' He broke off, grimacing, his eyes dropping away as if he couldn't bear to look at her. 'Believe me, the last thing on my mind was sex.'

Luisa's face was burning; pain and shame filled her. She stared into the garden without seeing it.

A joke? she thought, humiliated. That was all it was to him? A joke?

'It got out of hand,' he said in a low, rough voice. 'You're a nurse; you've probably had some sort of training in psychology—maybe you'll understand what happened in my head. One minute I was angry and kissed you simply because I knew you were sorry for me, and that made me furious. But just as I was going to let go of you again I thought of something else ... someone else ...'

She turned to stone. He had thought of someone else while he was kissing her? The insult went so deep that she felt tears burning behind her eyes.

'That's why I lost control,' he said, his voice hoarse. 'Crazy, really. It's stupid to keep thinking about it ... her ...'

Luisa was fighting not to let the tears escape, yet at the same time she was deeply intent on what he said. Her? Her? Who was he talking about?

'She isn't even real,' he muttered. 'I don't know her, at all. Not her name, where she lives, anything about her! I just saw her, once, from a distance, but ...' A sigh wrenched through him. 'But she haunts me. Can you understand that?'

'Yes,' she whispered through her own pain. 'Yes, I can understand that.' She understood it far better than he could guess. Ever since she first set eyes on him she had been haunted by his image and every day her obsession grew worse.

'Can you?' He looked at her doubtfully. 'I wish I did. If anyone had told me I would ever feel this way about a woman I hadn't even met I'd have laughed at him. It's some sort of sickness, but I can't cure myself. I know it's all in my own mind; it's just a mirage. I've told myself that a hundred times. You can't fall in love with a girl you haven't even spoken to—it's madness. After all, what do I know about her?' He turned restlessly, walked away, turned again, and walked back, his hands driven into the pockets of his well-worn blue jeans.

Luisa watched him, biting down on her inner lip to stop herself crying out, betraying herself.

Zachary laughed harshly. 'For all I know she's the biggest bore in the world! She may be as thick as a plank, an outrageous flirt, or just plain dull! She may be married with two children! I've thought of all the down-to-earth reasons why I should just forget about her, but I can't. She's in my dreams every night; I wake up thinking about her.'

Luisa had never known such pain was possible. The passion in his voice, the obsessed intensity of his pale face and the driven movements of his body made her so jealous that she wanted to scream.

'I only saw her once,' he repeated. 'Oddly enough . . .' He halted and turned to look at Luisa through half-veiled grey eyes, his lids lowered as if the light from the high studio windows hurt him.

'Oddly enough,' he repeated slowly, 'it was that evening—do you think that's coincidence, or that is why I can't forget her?'

Somehow Luisa managed to speak, her voice low, unsteady. 'Which evening?'

Their eyes met and as if they were in telepathic communication she knew the answer and before he said anything she whispered, 'The night of the accident?'

He nodded.

She breathed carefully, her mind in turmoil, trying to make some sense of what he was telling her.

'I was somewhere between Tareton and Whinbury,' he said, 'driving carefully, because I had my canvases in the back of the van and I didn't want them damaged. I was thinking about the exhibition, I remember. I was quite excited—it was going to be the most important I'd ever had—and I was on edge, too, I suppose, because of that. It was twilight, I'd got my headlights on because the light was so bad, and I was right out in the country; there were no street-lights. Then, just ahead, on my right, there was a blur of light...a whiteness floating along above a hedge...or a wall, maybe? I can't quite remember which. I was startled, anyway. I couldn't make out what it was; I instinctively hit the brakes and the car began to slow to a crawl.'

What on earth was he talking about? wondered Luisa, staring at him with puzzled dark blue eyes.

Meeting that gaze, he pulled a face. 'I know, it sounds crazy...but I thought...just for a second I thought...it was a ghost.'

'A ghost?' She looked incredulously at him. 'I wouldn't have thought you were the type to believe in them.'

'I'm not. And it wasn't, of course,' he said, flatly. 'But you know how the mind can play tricks, especially in the twilight, when things are grey and seem to be melting into the night. A very deceptive time of day. I did a double take, naturally. At once. And I laughed at myself—I didn't realise I had such a vivid imagination. What I'd seen was a girl.

Walking slowly along behind a hedge ... and it was a hedge, I remember now. A hedge with a large garden behind it, and somewhere in the distance I think there must have been a house. But I wasn't looking at anything but her. She looked as if she had always been there, moving through the twilight in that garden. She was wearing white, something loose and floating like a Victorian night-gown——'

Luisa's eyes opened wider, darkened incredulously. 'A nightgown? She was walking in the garden in a nightgown?'

He looked impatient, as if she was being stupid. 'I don't suppose it was one—it just looked like that. That's the whole point—it was all so strange, as if I was having a dream, as if it wasn't really happening at all.' He caught her eyes and frowned irritably. 'But it did happen; I wasn't imagining it...' he insisted, although she hadn't said a word. That had been what she was thinking, of course. The way he described it made her doubt that he had really seen anything at all. But she bit back any more questions and let him go on.

'One thing I am sure about—she was very young, a girl, barely out of childhood...' His eyes had a dreamy look to them and he stared into the distance as though he could see the girl again, in the pale winter sky, in his own bare garden.

Luisa watched him, a bitter ache inside her. Why couldn't he look like that for her? Why did he have to be fixated on someone he had only seen once and maybe had imagined anyway?

He didn't even look at her; he was blind to what she was thinking and feeling, far too wrapped up in his own emotions.

'She was slightly built,' he said. 'Small and slender, with the most amazing long, flowing black hair—a positive mane of it—blowing about as she moved. I could just see her face—it was like a cameo: finely etched features, delicate, rather pale. I slowed down until I stopped altogether and sat there, staring at her, but although she glanced in my direction I don't think she really noticed me; I sensed that she was totally wrapped up in her own thoughts.'

The irony of that made Luisa want to laugh out loud. The girl hadn't even looked at him, had been far too obsessed with her own thoughts?

Well, it was funny, wasn't it? Love was a merry-go-round, gaudily painted, with loud music and bright lights, all the fun of the fair! But the lovers endlessly chasing each other round and round never caught up with the beloved, and they themselves were being pursued by someone they never even looked at!

Zachary said with a frown, 'Somehow I got the feeling she wasn't happy...' He broke off and looked down at Luisa, smiled crookedly at her. 'Sorry to go on and on, but I haven't been able to talk to anyone about her all these months. I haven't even had a chance to go back and find her, because a few minutes after I'd seen her your father came round the corner and crashed right into me. Since then——' his face hardened, the scars livid and his eyes bitter '—I can't bear to drive a car again. No doubt I'll get over that phase one day, but at the moment I have to get taxis everywhere, or ask friends to drive me. I couldn't ask one of my friends to drive around the country lanes with me looking for a girl whose name I don't know. I'm not even sure where it was I saw her. Somewhere between Tareton and Whinbury, but that adds up to several miles of road. And then even if I did find her...well, look at me! How could I ask her out? Why would a girl as lovely as that want to go out with a guy who looks like me?'

'You really don't look as bad as you think...' she said huskily, and he scowled.

'Don't start that again! OK, you're the medical expert—tell me your diagnosis. Am I crazy? Suffering from delusions? Or what?'

Luisa managed a faint smile. 'Oh, I'm sure you saw a girl walking in a garden, and no doubt she was as pretty as you say she is...but what has fixed her in your mind was the fact that you had the accident so soon after. You've been very ill and you've had nothing to do but lie in bed and think. Once you're back to normal, and working, you'll forget her.' She glanced deliberately at her watch, pretending a start of surprise. 'Look at the time! I have to go, Mr West. I hope the police catch your burglars and you get your equipment back.'

He followed her to his front door. 'Thanks for helping clean the place up—I would still be hard at it if you hadn't come along.'

'That's OK,' she said casually. 'Goodbye.' The word had a bitter taste in her mouth. She said it lightly, but she meant it seriously, and it hurt to say it. Goodbye, my love, she thought as she walked towards her car.

'See you,' Zachary called after her, and she shivered. Not if she could help it.

CHAPTER SEVEN

THE New Year celebrations, as always, brought another wave of patients into the hospital, for one reason or another, mostly connected with drinking too much on New Year's Eve. Mostly they went to other wards—Surgical or a general ward—but there was always a crop of burns patients, too—the most poignant, as always, being the children. That year, Luisa was grateful to be kept busy. She couldn't brood over Zachary while she was being run off her feet on the ward, but the strain of trying not to think about him made her temper short, and her staff began eyeing her warily whenever they saw her coming.

Luisa caught that look on Anthea Carter's face one evening early in January as she advanced towards the younger girl, and grimaced. I'm turning into a gorgon! she thought, remembering her own first years in nursing and her dread of some of the older sisters. I must watch it!

'Have you done those injections, Nurse?' she asked in a gentler voice than she had been going to use.

Anthea looked flustered, but then that was her usual expression—she spent her days running and never catching up. 'I was just going to, Sister. I've been so busy that——'

125

'Well, get on with it now! And make a New Year resolution to keep to the schedule as far as possible, whatever the emergencies you have to deal with too.'

'Yes, Sister,' Anthea Carter said meekly. 'Have you made any New Year resolutions, Sister?'

Luisa gave her a dry smile. 'Yes, but I never talk about my resolutions in case I don't keep them. Get on with those injections now, Nurse. You don't have time to gossip, do you? You're behind with your work already.'

She watched the other girl go pink and scurry away like a worried mouse escaping from the cat. Poor Anthea—she led a hectic life. It was a pity to have to keep nagging at her, but what choice was there? The work had to be done and she had to learn to get on with it without being prodded.

Luisa went back to cope with her mountain of paperwork, her face rueful. She only had one New Year resolution—to forget Zachary West—and she couldn't have told Anthea Carter about that!

She stared down at a form she was filling out, not seeing it. David, she thought. What am I going to do about David? He was such a nice man and she enjoyed his company, but she knew she would never fall in love with him, and, without loving him, she couldn't sleep with him. She had waited too long for true love to accept second best now, much as she liked David.

For a long time now she'd half thought there was no such thing as the sort of love poets wrote about. There was sexual desire and there was affection, but so far, for her, the two had never come together. She had even wondered if she was capable of wanting a man so badly that she had to sleep with him, come hell or high water. Some men had accused her of being frigid, and Luisa had half believed them. Until now.

Meeting Zachary had shown her that she was capable of a desire so strong it was tearing her apart, which was why she knew she had to stop seeing David, because she would never feel that way about him.

The phone rang, making her jump. Not another emergency admission? They had one spare bed left, but it made her very nervous to have all her beds in use. It was tempting fate.

She picked up the phone, the fingers of her other hand crossed. 'Burns Unit; Sister Gilbey speaking.'

It was her father and she sighed in relief as she recognised his voice.

'Hello, Dad, how are you?'

'Don't ask,' he gloomily said. The Christmas spent in Switzerland had not done him much good. He had come back even more jumpy than he had been when he left. 'How about you? OK?'

'Busy,' she said, evasively. 'The usual result of Christmas and the New Year—a lot of new patients for all of us. Tonight I only have one bed available if we get a new arrival, and that's bad news. I can't talk long, Dad; we'll be settling the ward down for the night soon.'

'Of course. Quickly, then; it's ages since I saw you—how about lunch soon?' he asked. 'When do you have a day off?'

'I have two days off starting tomorrow,' she said slowly. She had intended to sleep all day because sleeping was something she hadn't been doing lately.

'How about lunch on Friday, then?' Harry Gilbey asked. 'I've had an offer I want to discuss with you.'

'Offer?'

Lowering his voice, he said, 'Somebody wants to buy the factory, and it may be a way out for me, but their offer is pitched very low and I suspect they've heard, somehow, that I'm in financial difficulties and they're getting in before anyone else can, and are hoping to pick up a bargain. I need to talk to you about it.'

'Dad, I know nothing about business. What about Noelle? What does she think?'

'I haven't told her yet,' Harry Gilbey admitted.

She was startled. 'Oh. I see.'

How many other secrets was he keeping from Noelle? What sort of marriage was it when there was so much hidden? His wife should be someone he could trust, go to for comfort and support when he was in trouble, not someone whose reactions he feared like this. Luisa frowned, doodling restlessly in the margin of her personal diary, which lay open on the desk. Her father wasn't happy, and that made her unhappy, too.

'I know what she'll say—she won't want me to sell,' Harry Gilbey muttered. 'I don't need to ask her opinion and I wouldn't get an unbiased reaction from her. At least I know you won't have an axe to grind; you'll listen and tell me honestly what you think and ... Luisa, I need to talk to someone; who else can I trust?'

'OK, Dad,' she said soothingly. 'Friday, then. Where?'

'Same place as before? The Cherry Tree? Now that the Christmas rush is over it's easier to get a reservation there.'

'Great, the food is terrific. Twelve-thirty?'

'Yes, I'll see you there at twelve-thirty,' he agreed, and rang off.

Luisa heard David's voice outside and hurried out to find out why he was on the ward at this hour, when he should have finished operating and gone home.

He was talking to Anthea Carter, who darted discreetly away as soon as Luisa appeared.

David gave her a weary smile. 'Have you got time for some cocoa? I'm low on blood sugar; this has been a long day.'

'You should go home to bed,' she said, but made him a mug of cocoa and got biscuits out of the ward biscuit tin.

'I'm too tired to sleep,' he said, grey-faced. 'And, anyway, I've got some days off coming up—starting Friday. You're off on Friday too, aren't you? Can we have dinner? At the Cherry Tree?'

She hesitated, and he gave her an odd, frowning look. 'Or are you busy doing something else?'

She didn't want to make a date with him, yet how could she break off their relationship here and now? She had to get him on his own, away from the hospital.

'No, it's just that on Friday I'm going to the Cherry Tree for lunch——'

'Who with?' he asked sharply.

'My father,' she said, disturbed by the note of jealousy in his voice. Their relationship had never shown signs of any intensity on either side before.

Now, when she was thinking of ending it, was not the time for David to change and become possessive or difficult.

He gave her a level stare, leaning back in his chair. 'I was afraid I had a rival! You'd tell me if you were dating someone else, wouldn't you? I'd hate to hear it on the grapevine.'

'I wouldn't do that to you,' she soberly said. 'If I start dating anyone else you'll be the first to hear.'

'It isn't surprising that I'm suspicious, though, when you refuse to sleep with me!' he accused, and hot colour ran up her face.

'David! Nurse Carter's next door in the linen room—keep your voice down.'

'Damn Carter,' he muttered, but in a lower tone. 'We've got to talk about this, Luisa. I didn't expect you to jump into bed with me on our first date—we both know where promiscuity leads...but we'll have been seeing each other for a year soon. You must see that we can't go on like this. I don't want to be your brother; I want to be your lover.'

She bit her lip. He was forcing this scene on her, in spite of her wish to spare him a public discussion.

'David, please...can we talk about this on Friday evening?'

'You always avoid the subject!' he furiously muttered, his hands clenched as if he wanted to do something violent. 'I'm beginning to think I've wasted my time with you; we're not getting anywhere, are we? I don't think you give a damn about me!'

She stiffened, all the colour going out of her face. 'I'm sorry, David,' she whispered. 'I never meant to hurt you. We'd better stop seeing each other.'

He looked at her incredulously, his face tense. 'Are you telling me you want to break up?'

She couldn't get a word out; she just nodded, her fingers twisting in her lap.

David stared at her, his mouth a tight white line, then got up and walked away in fast strides, the ward door swinging violently after he went through it.

The following day Luisa slept and slept as if she were drugged although she hadn't taken anything but a cup of hot milk when she got home from the hospital. She had been too tired to eat. She took off her clothes, automatically folded them for laundering, put on her nightdress, fell into bed and was asleep in minutes.

She had the strangest dream—she was walking in a garden in the half-light of dusk when suddenly she saw Zachary running towards her. Her heart turned over and she was filled with happiness. But as he reached her he stopped dead, stared, then scowled and said, 'You're not her! I don't want you!' Turning angrily away, he vanished, and Luisa stood there, tears in her eyes, stricken.

She woke up in darkness, and was thrown into panic. It had been about nine-thirty when she went to sleep—she couldn't have slept the day away, surely?

But when she switched on her bedside lamp to look at her alarm clock she discovered that it was, indeed, nearly seven o'clock in the evening. She had slept for over nine hours!

Normally she hoped to sleep for five, at most six hours. More than nine was a record! She slid her feet to the floor, pushed them into her slippers, and put on her dressing-gown. First she made herself a cup of coffee and drank it reading the newspaper she had found waiting for her when she got home, then she went to have a shower and dress.

It was much too late now to consider going out for a meal in a restaurant, or to see a film, as she sometimes did on her nights off, so she started to cook a risotto. It was one of her favourite meals because it was so easy to cook, a one-pan affair which also used up any left-overs she found in her tiny fridge. Sometimes there were scraps of chicken, or fish, but today she only had some sweetcorn, red and green peppers, tinned kidney beans, and tomatoes.

While she was turning this into a delicious meal, the phone rang. She turned the heat off and went to answer the phone.

'Oh, you're in!' David's curt voice said, making her jump. 'Can I come round? We have to talk, Luisa; we can't just let it end like this.'

She was thrown into confusion. 'David... I... Look, maybe tomorrow we could meet...?'

'No, now,' he said tersely, and put down the phone.

He was coming here. She bit her lip, disturbed by the anger in his voice. She couldn't blame him for being furious with her, but neither could she do anything about her own feelings. She liked him, but not enough—what else could she say but tell him they had no future together? She had never made him any promises. Their relationship had begun casually and had always had to fit into their busy working lives; there had never been any intensity on either side. Oh, David had wanted her

to sleep with him, but he had never told her he loved
her, or asked if she loved him.

All the same, she was nervous about him coming
here tonight, in that mood. Male violence worried
her.

She slowly walked back to check on her risotto
and the phone rang again. She ran to answer it this
time. Maybe David had changed his mind?

It wasn't him. 'This is Zachary West,' the familiar deep voice said.

Her heart turned over in that sickening roll of
excitement. 'Oh, hello,' she said huskily.

His voice was brusque. 'Look, I can't get hold
of my own doctor—he's out somewhere on an
emergency call—but I need advice... I've had a
terrific headache all day and the usual pills aren't
doing a thing to help. I wondered... have you got
anything stronger? Or should I just take a double
dose of my sleeping pills and try to sleep until the
headache's gone?'

'No, don't do that,' she said, frowning. A terrific headache? All day? Which normal medication
couldn't shift? That sounded rather worrying. 'If
there is anything seriously wrong that could be
dangerous,' she told him. 'I think I'd better come
and have a look at you, make a few checks. It could
be nothing and it could be something that a doctor
ought to see. Best to be sure. I'll be with you in
half an hour.'

'I suppose I hoped you'd say that, or I wouldn't
have rung you,' he wryly murmured. 'I'm sorry to
bother you, but thanks, anyway.'

'That's OK,' she said, smiling, warmth filling her,
and rang off.

Her risotto was perfectly cooked. She turned it into a plastic bowl with a lid which she snapped fast. She would take it with her. She could re-heat it at Zachary's house if she had to wait for a doctor to arrive.

She quickly put on some make-up, put her black hair up into its usual chignon, then put on her red jacket, and went out to her car. As she drove away she saw David's car heading that way. She avoided eye contact, hoping he wouldn't spot her car, but as she turned the corner she saw his car swing round in the road to point the way she had gone.

Oh, no! He's following me! she thought, biting her lip. There was quite a bit of traffic, and no break in it for her to get out. She should have waited to let a lumbering lorry go by, but she took the risk of shooting out in front of it. She heard the driver angrily hoot, but she was already driving fast to get away before David's car reached the corner.

When she glanced back a few moments later there was no sign of him so she relaxed and let herself think about Zachary, anxiety filling her at once.

What could the headache mean? He had had head injuries during the accident, but they had not been serious, as far as she remembered, and there was very little about Zachary that she had forgotten.

It could have no connection with the accident, of course. It could be psychologically prompted. He was obviously very upset about being unable to paint. Maybe the headache was the way his subconscious dealt with the pressure of constantly trying and failing?

She took just under half an hour to reach the cottage. She had brought a bag of equipment she had gathered together over the years: thermometer, blood-pressure unit, a few basic medicines. While she was getting the bag out of the car she heard the screech of tyres and straightened, looking round in some alarm.

For a crazy second she almost thought David's car might drive right over her, then he screamed to a stop, inches from her car bonnet.

He got out, slammed his car door, and advanced, face dark with rage. 'Why did you go out when you knew I was coming round? What the hell are you playing at?'

Pale, Luisa stammered, 'I'm sorry, David, I had an emergency call.'

'What?' He looked round at the Queen Anne cottage, the remote landscape. 'Out here? What are you talking about?' And then the front door opened. David's face stiffened as he saw Zachary West standing there. 'That's... I know him—he was one of my patients... The artist... What's his name...?'

'Zachary West,' Luisa huskily said.

David stared at Zachary, who was walking towards them along the path, then turned slowly and looked down at her.

'What is going on? He called and asked you to come?' His voice rose, getting angrier. 'Why should he do that? Why not his own doctor? And how did he get your home phone number? Have you been seeing him since he was in your ward?'

Her colour coming and going, she could only stammer and make herself look guiltier than she was. 'Well... in a w... in a way... but...'

Zachary reached them and her voice died. She looked at him pleadingly. 'I was just explaining...'

'Explaining what?' Zachary asked, his black brows lifting arrogantly, and David looked at him with deep dislike.

'You, Mr West—she was trying to explain you—and why you should have rung her, not your own doctor.' His mouth twisted into an angry sneer. 'And not being very convincing about it.'

Zachary stared back at him with equal hostility. 'I did ring my own doctor; he was out on an emergency.'

'Why couldn't you wait until he came back? Why ring Sister Gilbey?' David looked him up and down, then snapped, 'What was so urgent? You don't look like an emergency case to me.'

'I had a headache,' Zachary said softly.

'A headache?' David's voice thickened with rage. 'You had a headache?' He seemed to be barely capable of speaking coherently, his face red and his body shaking with temper. 'You had a headache, so you rang her and she came rushing over here, forgetting everything else.' He turned slowly and looked down at Luisa, who was so horrified by this scene that she couldn't get a word out to placate him or make him understand how worried she had been about Zachary's headache. Somehow she sensed that it would not ring true when David could see Zachary for himself. Zachary did not look as if he was at death's door.

After a long pause, David said coldly, 'Well, that more or less explains everything, doesn't it? I get the picture at last. A pity you couldn't tell me until now. I wasted a lot of time misunderstanding what was going on between us. You must have been laughing at me——'

'No, David,' she cried unhappily, seeing the expression in his eyes. 'You've got it wrong, believe me!'

'I don't think so,' he said with a grim little smile.

'David, I wouldn't want to hurt you for worlds!' she protested, and he met her anxious dark blue eyes and stared into them in silence for a moment.

'I believe you. Most men wouldn't. But I know what a soft heart you've got, Luisa. I wish you'd told me the truth, though.'

Then he turned and walked away, got into his car, and drove off while she watched him, hating herself.

He was right. She should have told him that she was in love with another man. She shouldn't have let their relationship drag on and on for months when she knew it really had no future.

'I gather that was your boyfriend?' Zachary murmured into the silence, and she turned and looked at him with immense resentment.

'Perhaps you'd like to explain how you came to cure the incurable headache, Mr West?' she furiously demanded.

He gave her a twisted little smile. 'It seems to have gone.'

'Gone?' she repeated shrilly, very flushed.

'Yes, amazing, isn't it? One minute I was almost blind with pain, then I heard your car and opened the door to find you and that guy having a violent row. I didn't know what was going on—I thought at first that he had run into the back of your car, or you had cut him up at a junction, something like that. I started to come out to back you up, then I realised the two of you knew each other, that it was a lot more personal than I'd suspected. He looked at me as if I were a slug he'd found in his lettuce, and you were stammering away like a schoolgirl, making excuses for having come over here.'

Angrily she snapped, 'You weren't much help, were you? You might at least have told him that you'd given me the impression you might be really ill.'

'I began to,' he protested, 'but he cut me off and started shouting at you, and anyway...' Unbelievably, he grinned at her. 'By then my headache was so much better that I had a feeling he might refuse to believe a word I said.'

Luisa couldn't deny that he was probably right. David would have thought he was lying, because Zachary did not look as if he was at death's door. His colour was far too good, his eyes very bright.

'I'm finding it hard myself,' she said icily. 'The miraculous cure doesn't quite ring true, Mr West.'

His grin went and his face tightened. He gave her a fixed stare. 'It is true, however,' he insisted. 'I don't know why my headache eased off suddenly like that, but it did. Maybe the adrenalin of finding myself in the middle of a violent row was what I needed?'

'Oh!' she gasped, feeling like hitting him. 'How about another one, then? I feel like having a violent row with you!'

He gave her a teasing, sideways look. 'That sounds promising!'

A pulse began to beat in Luisa's throat. She couldn't hold his gaze and had to look away.

'You've just been wasting my time,' she muttered, lashes down over her eyes.

'Sorry about that,' he said blithely, not sounding at all sorry. 'I've been doing nothing but mope about for days—maybe I bored myself into having a headache. Until the accident I was always very busy, from morning till night—I worked full-out during daylight hours. Since I came out of hospital I've pottered around the house doing odd jobs, but I haven't been using my mind at all. Maybe it rebelled?'

'And maybe you exaggerated when you told me your symptoms!'

'No, I didn't! The pain was so bad I felt like banging my head on a wall.'

She believed the insistence with which he said it, but she was still angry.

'I still don't know why you didn't tell David the truth—whether he believed you or not—instead of letting him drive off like that! Didn't you think you owed it to me, under the circumstances? It was all your fault, after all.'

'I might have done if I hadn't got the distinct impression that you wouldn't be heartbroken to split up with him,' he drawled, and her colour rose in a hot wave.

'You know nothing about it!'

'I have eyes and ears and if you had really wanted to talk him round you would have done.'

She bit her lip. He was far too perceptive, and that was worrying. He might start picking up other things from her; Luisa was terrified of him guessing how she felt about him. The humiliation would be more than she could bear.

'Well, anyway, you obviously don't need me, so I'll be on my way,' she said, turning back towards her car.

He caught her arm. 'Don't go.'

She looked up, startled, dark blue eyes wary.

Zachary's smile was almost boyish: half rueful, half pleading. 'I haven't talked to anyone for days. Have you eaten? I haven't got much in the house, but I could cook egg and bacon, or an omelette. Don't leave me alone, Luisa.'

It was the first time he had ever used her first name, and she registered it with a sort of shock, but said huskily, 'I ought to get back.'

She wanted badly to stay, yet was afraid of getting hurt even more than she had been. He was in love with another woman. His interest in her was purely platonic. He needed company and she was better than nobody. It was no compliment.

'You can stay for an hour or so, surely?' he said, taking her bag out of her hand. 'What's in here? Instruments of torture?'

'Medical equipment. I thought I might need to do some tests on you.' She tried to take it back, but he held the bag at arm's length.

'Well, you can do your tests and make sure the headache won't return, can't you? Then I'll cook you a little supper.'

'I brought food with me,' she said, rather embarrassed. 'I had just cooked a risotto when you rang, so I brought it with me. I thought I might re-heat it here if I had to stay for any length of time— wait for an ambulance, for instance...'

He gazed at her, eyes narrowed. 'You thought I might be that ill?'

'It's wise to be prepared for any emergency. You sounded as if you were at death's door.'

'I felt that way at the time,' he said, mouth crooked. 'Is your risotto in here too?' he asked, still holding her bag.

'Yes.' She gave up. OK, he was using her for entertainment because he was bored. He would much rather be with another woman. That hurt, but he still needed her, she couldn't help feeling moved by his loneliness—and, too, there was her guilt over the accident. She blamed herself for it. If she hadn't rung her father and emotionally blackmailed him into driving back in a hurry he wouldn't have crashed into Zachary, and Zachary would not be suffering headaches because he was unable to work any more.

But all the excuses she came up with meant nothing compared to the real truth. She wanted to be with him; it made her happy just to look at him and hear his voice—why shouldn't she be happy for a little while? Even if it was all illusory, a fool's paradise? He need never guess; she certainly wouldn't tell him and she could surely manage to hide her feelings for this one evening?

'It should stretch to two, unless you're very hungry,' she said in a cool, steady voice, and he smiled at her, making her heart turn over at the difference a smile could make to that dark, scarred face. Did he really believe himself to be ugly, repulsive to women? If he knew what he did to her when he looked at her like that he'd realise how crazy that idea was!

'We can eat some fruit as a dessert,' he suggested, going into the cottage, with Luisa following him. 'The kitchen is this way... I had some apples, oranges and bananas in my delivery this morning. I have my food delivered from the village twice a week—they charge me for the convenience, but it's worth it. That way I don't have to see people's faces when I walk down the street. The shopkeeper is used to my face now; he's stopped staring and then trying not to look at me. That's what I hate most— the people who do a double take then very obviously pretend they can't see me.'

She winced and shook her head at him. 'You really are imagining all this! Your face is scarred, but not that badly now.'

He reached out suddenly and took her hand.

Luisa stiffened, her fingers trembling in his grip.

Watching her, Zachary lifted her hand to his face. 'Feel it... go on, feel it... and then tell me it isn't badly scarred.'

Her mouth dry, she ran her fingertips along his cheek, feeling the indentations of the scars under her skin, the prickle of shaved hair, the clenched impatience of his jaw.

She couldn't look into his eyes in case he saw what touching him was doing to her. She stared instead at his cheek, his jaw, his mouth, and desire turned her legs weak and made heat pulse through her body.

Huskily, she murmured, 'They make you look rather piratical, a dangerous man to cross!' And she laughed, risking a brief look up, into his eyes, then wished she hadn't.

He was watching her so intently. Did he suspect the churning sensuality inside her? Colour flared in her cheeks as he softly said, 'But I want to look sexy! Not piratical.'

You do, she thought, swallowing, aching to let her fingers slide across his mouth.

'I notice you aren't going to tell me I do!' he mocked her, then, 'Your fingers are so cool and soothing.'

She snatched them away and he laughed.

Suddenly exasperated, Luisa said, 'I'm starving. I'd better reheat the risotto.' She looked around the kitchen, exclaiming, 'Oh, you've got a new microwave oven! Or did the police catch the burglar and get it back for you?'

He shook his head, his expression wry, knowing she was deliberately changing the subject, trying to lighten the charged atmosphere between them.

'This is a new one. I find they save so much time and trouble that I rang the shop in Whinbury where I'd bought the first one and asked them to bring me an identical oven. It had taken me so long to discover how the first one worked that I didn't want to have to start all over again with a different oven.'

'Well, I can reheat the risotto in a few minutes in it.' The kitchen was modern and brightly lit, the walls painted pale yellow and the fittings made of golden pine.

There was a pine table and chairs, too. 'Shall we eat in here?' Zachary asked, and she nodded.

'First I must check your blood-pressure and pulse, then if they're OK we'll eat,' she said, opening her bag.

He sat down on a chair by the table and she took his pulse; it was a little fast, but not disturbingly so. His blood-pressure was raised, too, but again she wasn't too worried by it, or by his temperature, which was almost normal.

'Nothing to worry about there,' she told him, getting up.

Soberly he said, 'I'm sorry to have brought you out on a wild-goose chase. Honestly.'

She washed her hands at the sink, her back to him. 'Forget it. I think you're probably right and your headaches are caused by boredom and inactivity. You must somehow get back to work, Mr West.'

'Zachary,' he said. 'You can't keep calling me Mr West, Luisa.'

She looked at the microwave controls a little fixedly, glad to have her back to him. They were simple enough; she took off the lid and slid the risotto into the oven, but didn't start the heating process yet. 'Would you lay the table, please? This will only take four minutes. Have you any salad?'

They worked together harmoniously, without speaking much, and ten minutes later were sitting down to their meal.

'Delicious,' Zachary said, as he took the empty plates to the dishwasher, which the burglars had not taken, probably because it would have taken time to detach it from the wall, and it was rather too large to be portable. 'I've never eaten a vegetable risotto before. Your own recipe?'

'I just chuck in whatever I have.'

'You're a good cook. I suppose I should have expected you would be, with your training.'

Her eyebrows rose. 'What has being a nurse got to do with cooking? We aren't taught to cook.'

'You need to be very calm and patient, though, and that is essential for a cook.'

'I wouldn't say that. One of the top chefs in London was a patient of mine once, and he was very temperamental. He was in hospital because he had a violent row in the kitchen with a Chinese chef—they ended up throwing things at each other, and my patient was on the receiving end of a meat cleaver. He'd thrown a carving knife at the Chinese, but missed.'

Zachary laughed. 'You're pulling my leg!'

'No,' she said, watching him peel an orange, his long brown fingers deft. A strange little quiver ran through her. He had the sexiest hands she had ever seen: just watching them made her go weak at the knees.

'Aren't you going to have some fruit?' he asked, looking up, and she hurriedly looked down, reaching for an apple.

'Yes, of course.' To change the subject she said, 'Have you thought of hypnosis? A good hypnotist might be able to help you clear the mental block which is stopping you from working.'

'Do you think so?' He frowned. 'I'm not sure I like the idea of being hypnotised—there's something creepy about it. Having your head invaded by someone else.'

'Under hypnosis you won't tell him anything you really don't want him to know, or do anything you really don't want to do,' she assured him. 'It works, just as acupuncture really works. I had a friend who had bad asthma; conventional medication could help the symptoms, but she had to keep taking stronger and stronger doses. Long-term, that was dangerous. She was advised to have acupuncture by one of our doctors at the hospital, who had a friend in general practice who practised acupuncture with some of his patients. Within a couple of months my friend was off medication altogether. Oh, she has occasional outbreaks, when she's under strain, but the acupuncture always works and doesn't have the same risks as conventional medicine.'

'I wouldn't have expected to get advice like that from a hospital nurse!'

'Oh, these days we have learnt that some alternative medicine can be very helpful.'

'Well, I'll think about it seriously, then,' he said. 'Now, I'll make the coffee; you go into the sitting-room and relax by the fire.'

She wandered into the sitting-room, which was shadowy, only one lamp lit, beside the couch facing the log fire crackling in the grate. There was a marvellous, resiny scent from the burning logs. Luisa picked up a book lying open on an arm of the couch. Zachary was reading a paperback copy of a famous Victorian travel book. She sat down and glanced through it with interest.

'I hope you haven't lost my page,' he said beside her suddenly, making her jump.

'No, you're on page seventy-three,' she said, flushing as she put the book down, open at that page. 'Are you enjoying it?'

'Very much. Victorian travellers must have been very tough, going such amazing distances on horseback or walking, through African bush, with so few medicines and risking some pretty horrific diseases.'

'They had to be tough to survive life in their own homes, with typhoid and cholera rife for most of the century,' she said drily. 'Even the Queen's husband died of typhoid, after all. The doctors couldn't save him.'

He grinned. 'I might have realised you'd know all about medical history! A trip into the unknown was just a little more dangerous than their daily lives here, in fact.'

'You're exaggerating again!' she said, laughing.

'Are you calling me a liar, woman?' he asked in mock ferocity, straightening to hand her a cup of coffee.

The firelight threw his shadow up on to the ceiling—huge, black, dominating—and Luisa's breath caught. He filled the room as he had already filled her life. Nothing in the world mattered to her except him.

CHAPTER EIGHT

THAT night the moon was full. Zachary West hadn't bothered to close his curtains before he got into bed, and moonlight slid across his face, disturbing his sleep with strange dreams.

He was in his car, driving down a shadowy road, not knowing where he was going, yet somehow waiting: waiting for someone, something to happen. Suddenly there she was—the girl in white, the wraith he had been pursuing in his dreams for months now. She was always just out of sight, never close enough to touch, floating through a garden in blue and mauve twilight, silent as a leaf drifting down from a tree in autumn, languorous as a breath, a sigh.

In the reasonless logic of dreams, Zachary found himself out of his car next, walking in the garden, too, calling her, but very distressed because he didn't know her name, he couldn't call her by name, so how would she know it was her he was looking for?

It seemed vital. If only he knew her name, he thought, hurrying along a path. He had a feeling he did know it, had simply forgotten it at this moment; it was on the tip of his tongue! He searched his memory over and over again, but the name escaped him.

He couldn't see her now; she wasn't in the garden any more. He kept stopping and looking around, calling . . . His voice echoed back from the trees like bird call, but the girl in white had vanished. He didn't give up. He had to find her. He kept running and calling, feverishly searching everywhere. Once or twice he thought he caught a glimpse of her black hair between leaves, heard the rustle of her long white dress whisking out of sight behind the trees.

He came out of the trees to find himself close to the house, which shimmered in the moon like a mirage. Zachary stopped on the edge of a green lawn, staring up at rows of blank windows.

The moonlight turned them all into mirrors, reflecting back the garden, himself. Zachary was about to walk away, back through the garden, when a shape appeared at one of the downstairs windows, framed between long, full curtains: a lovely face, dreamy blue eyes which watched him. His heart leapt. It was her!

He could see her clearly: the flowing dark hair, the pure cameo of a face, the frail girl's figure in a long white dress. She put her hands out to him, her full sleeves billowing. He hurried towards the house, beginning to run with eagerness. At last he was going to see her face to face!

Before he reached the house, though, there was a sound like gunfire and, while he stared in shock, white-painted shutters slammed shut one by one over every window in the house until he could see nothing; the house was blind, completely shut up.

He ran to the front door and began hammering on it, but, even while he called her and banged down the big brass lion's head knocker, he was coming up out of sleep like a deep-sea diver surfacing far too fast, his body shuddering and shaking.

For a second he was seized with fear and panic; he couldn't remember where he was, what had happened. Then he heard familiar sounds, the tide rolling up on to the beach below the house, the cry of gulls in the dawn light, the whine of the winter wind.

He rolled over, groaning, to look at the clock. Seven o'clock. The night was more or less over, but Zachary felt as weary as if he hadn't slept at all. He lay there frowning, thinking about that last dream and trying to work out what it had meant. Why had the shutters come down on the house, excluding him?

Because she isn't for you, a little voice said inside his head. Don't you understand? You have to forget her. That's the meaning of the dream. Search as you like; you'll never find her, never get any closer.

Angrily he got out of bed into the faint chill of dawn. Dreams! What did they mean, anyway? One day he would go and look for her, and he was certain he would find her, that she would be waiting.

Walking across the room, naked, he caught sight of himself in the mirror, his body tense with frustration, and bleakly inspected himself. If you ignored the face, he looked perfectly normal again: shoulders smooth, unmarked by the fire, his chest showing that wedge of dark hair growing downwards to his stomach, which was still flat, in spite of his months of inertia in bed, because he had worked at staying fit as soon as he was out of hospital.

He had spent time in Provence with Flora and her family, last autumn, walking and swimming and playing tennis, and the tan he had picked up then still lingered. Even his face was looking better as the new skin grafts weathered and the scars faded, and if the plastic surgeon was being truthful the next operation should be the last. There should be no more visible scars; his face should look more or less as it had done before the accident.

But how could he ask a girl so much younger than himself, with that pure cameo of a face which breathed innocence and sweetness to...?

No! He couldn't, ever. Tense and pale, he turned fiercely away from his reflection. After a shower, dressed in jeans and a thick blue fisherman's sweater, his feet pushed into old yachting shoes with non-slip rope soles, he had breakfast. A cup of strong coffee, an orange, then he went into his studio to stare at the blank canvas on the easel.

He knew now what he wanted to paint. Perhaps if he painted her, he would stop dreaming about her? Or perhaps he would find her?

Luisa didn't sleep well, either, with the moonlight trickling through her curtains, and what sleep she did get was broken into fragmented dreams of Zachary. She had never had such strange dreams— erotic, disturbing, making her shift and twist in her warm bed, her body trembling. Yet she did not want to wake up, and when she did, each time, she could have cried with disappointment because she always woke up at the wrong moment.

She dreamt she was on a beach with Zachary, who was lying beside her asleep on glittering, blindingly white sand. She was awake, lying on her side, her head propped on one hand, watching him. She couldn't take her eyes off him. He was wearing

an open black shirt and jeans and looked intensely
sexy. Then he shifted, yawning, and his eyes
opened. He smiled at her and she felt a deep happiness; she knew he was going to say something . . . something   important,   something
wonderful . . .

Then she woke up. Sighed. Looked at the clock.
Three in the morning! She lay awake, thinking of
Zachary, then slowly went back to sleep.

Some time that night she dreamt of being on the
beach with Zachary, again, but this time he was
wearing nothing but a pair of black swimming
briefs, and mirror-lensed sunglasses. The sun
poured down over his gleaming gold-skinned body.
She was dry-mouthed with desire.

'Touch me, Luisa,' he whispered, sending shock
waves of panic through her body. She woke up, still
trembling, yet aching with frustration because she
hadn't touched him. Oh, why had she woken up
just then?

She was awake for quite a while that time, her
mind obsessed with images from her dreams, but
finally fell asleep again, and dreamt of running
through the surf and waves of a southern sea, blue
sky above, blue water all around her, and the gulls
crying overhead.

It dawned on her that she was totally naked only
as she realised that someone was chasing her. She
heard him splashing behind her. She looked over
her shoulder, laughing, and Zachary was there. He
was naked, too, and a flash of desire crackled between them.

He caught up with her, his body wet and smooth
against her own as he flung his arms around her.

She felt his fingers, cool and caressing on her naked breast, and desire pierced her. She moaned with pleasure, and stumbled, fell into the blue sea. Zachary fell with her; they rolled over and over in the waves, then she was lying under him, sand grating on her back, her hair floating on the sea like strange weed, and Zachary's head came down, blotting out the sun, darkening the sky. Luisa had never known such an intense sensuality as she felt when his mouth closed round her breast, his legs entangling with her own, his skin wetly sliding on hers. She moved restlessly, eagerly, as his body crushed her down, the sound of the sea in their ears mingling with the sound of their own thick breathing. She lifted her mouth to hunt for his, clasping his wet head in her hands.

A second later she was awake, trembling and aching, ready to weep because she had not wanted the dream to end.

By then it was nearly day; she got up and sat in her little kitchen with a cup of coffee, watching the sky clear and another wintry day begin. The sooner she went back to work the better, she thought grimly. At least when she was hard at work she couldn't keep thinking, or dreaming, about Zachary West.

She had lunch with her father. It was very cold; she shivered as she got out of her car to walk to the restaurant. A few snowflakes blew in the north wind, settling on her hair and coat. She was glad to get indoors. The bar area was already crowded and a wave of warm air met her as she pushed open the door.

Her father waved, smiling, but as she took off her coat and handed it to the hovering waiter she noted how weary and lined her father's face was. He had aged years since the accident.

But she managed a cheerful grin, joining him. 'Hello, Dad, sorry I'm late—I got held up in traffic. What are you drinking? No, I won't have that; I'll have a glass of white wine, please.'

The waiter ambled off without hurrying, took her coat to the tiny cloakroom before going to get her drink. Luisa settled back against the leather seat, picking up the menu her father had been reading.

'Isn't this weather miserable? My fingers are quite blue with cold,' she said, glancing down the list of food. 'This is a day for soup, I think—broth, delicious. Then I'll have the salmon *en croûte*—that sounds good. What are you having, Dad?'

'Oh, I don't mind; I'll eat whatever you're eating,' he said without interest, and Luisa gave him a concerned sideways glance.

'How are you, Dad?'

'Fine,' he said, unconvincingly.

She sighed. 'And Noelle? How's she?'

'Busy.' The lines on his face seemed to deepen. 'She's good at business, Luisa; she gets a real kick out of it. I used to have her enthusiasm, but it's gone now.' He gave a sigh.

The waiter came back with her drink and took their order, proffering a wine list. Her father accepted it and ran a quick eye over the pages, then ordered one of his favourite French wines—a Montlouis white from the Loire region.

Only when they had settled at their table did he mention the sale of the factory. 'It's a firm offer and I might not get a better one, not in the present economic climate, Luisa, and it would be an immediate injection of cash just in case I have to pay West a huge sum in damages.'

She frowned. 'Wouldn't it be wiser to wait until after the case is over? It would give you more time to find a better buyer.'

'That's not very likely.'

'Dad, you're being so defeatist! I really think you should consult Noelle and your accountants before you make any decisions, anyway, but there is another point—if you put a higher value on the factory and don't sell it at this much lower figure then when the case does come to court you will have better assets on paper.'

Harry Gilbey gave her a startled look, then laughed, his face lightening a little. 'You're very shrewd. A pity you didn't come into the business instead of becoming a nurse.'

Uncertainly, she frowned. 'You never said you wanted me to do that, Dad. When I told you I wanted to be a nurse you encouraged me to enter training.'

'It's an admirable profession, darling. Don't look so worried. I didn't really expect you to join me in the business, anyway.' A wry smile twitched his lips. 'I suppose I had an old-fashioned notion about girls not being good at business. I expected you would get married soon, and maybe pick someone who might want to join me in the firm; that was the full extent of my thinking where you were concerned. I've learned a lot since then, especially since I married Noelle. As my secretary she was efficient and down-to-earth, but once she was my wife she changed radically. I'd been blind about her true nature, Luisa.' His eyes were sad and resigned. 'She is a very ambitious and hard-headed woman.'

'Yes,' Luisa said. She was deeply sorry for her father's disillusionment about Noelle; she would far rather have seen him happy and contented in his marriage, even though she had never liked her stepmother.

Grimacing, Harry Gilbey said, 'To tell the truth, I'm scared stiff of telling her about the offer for the factory. She's going to make my life hell when she knows we're in financial trouble.'

Luisa frowned thoughtfully. 'I wonder. If she's as good at business as you say she is, she must have some idea of how things are. Put your cards on the table, Dad; tell her the truth. I think you owe it to her. After all, she is your wife. She has the right to know the truth about how things stand.'

They spent the rest of the meal arguing about it, but in the end she managed to persuade him to broach the subject to Noelle that evening.

'And it might be best if you don't tell her you've discussed it with me,' she advised, and got a bleak little smile from her father.

'No doubt you're right. I won't even mention you. I'm sorry you and she don't get on, though. She can be difficult.' He gave a long sigh. 'Marriage is a difficult relationship, darling. When you get around to it, think hard before you make up your mind.'

'I will, don't worry!'

'Are you still seeing that doctor, what's his name? David?'

She shook her head.

'I'm sorry,' her father said, watching her with sympathy. 'I liked him; he seemed a good man.'

'He is, but we weren't . . . it didn't——'

'Never mind,' Harry Gilbey quickly said, seeing she was upset. 'One day your prince will come, darling.'

As she let herself into her flat later she kept hearing his voice in her head. One day your prince will come . . . prince will come . . .

Zachary West was no prince, and he certainly wasn't hers, but she wished she could have talked to her father about him. She wished she could talk to someone about him, about the way she felt, but she didn't have that outlet. She had listened to her father talking unhappily about Noelle, how much he still loved her, yet how uncertain he knew his hold on her to be—but she had not breathed a word to him about how her own tangled and bitter emotions. He was the last person she could talk to about Zachary, in the circumstances!

Her father rang her next day, sounding quite buoyant. 'I told Noelle last night, and you were absolutely right, darling; she wasn't surprised.'

'Well, I suspected she would have some idea!' Luisa said drily.

'I could kick myself for not having talked to her before,' said Harry Gilbey. 'She said she'd realised we had a problem, that that was why she had been working so hard to put the firm back on to a solid basis. She thought we would get a better price for it, if we did have to sell, if it was a going concern rather than one that was losing money.'

'I'm sure she's right,' Luisa said slowly, realising she would have to revise her opinion of Noelle.

'But she doesn't want to take this offer. She has been doing business with a man in Birmingham who has a chain of shops all over the north of England. We manufacture various items for his shops, and she thinks he might be ready to inject some capital, become a partner. He wants to expand down south and is also interested in owning some of his suppliers, to cut his costs.'

'Do you like the idea?' Luisa asked, frowning.

'Well, I think I'd like to retire. I'm bored with the business, I've worked most of my life—it's time to relax. Play more golf!'

'But won't you be bored, Dad?' she anxiously asked.

'I've been bored with the business for a long time.' He shrugged. 'If I get fed up with being in retirement I can always come back, but at the moment I have a few good years ahead of me— I'm still fit and active. I shall enjoy not having to do a nine-to-five job six days a week!'

'So you aren't just doing this to raise capital to pay damages to Zachary West?' she said, feeling slightly easier, and her father shook his head.

'Noelle is right, you know. I lost interest in the business before I even met her. I shall be quite happy to take a back seat and let Noelle and this other man take over. Apparently, Noelle plans to be in charge of the day-to-day running of the company while our new partner will only take an occasional interest so long as she is successful and he is satisfied with profits.'

'I'm sure Noelle will be very successful,' Luisa said, and her father smiled and nodded wryly.

'I'm sure she will be, too!'

*   *   *

It was difficult, working with David, when she went back on night duty. He was perfectly polite, of course. David wasn't the type to bear malice or be rude, but there was a frost in his manner whenever they met and Luisa found it painful, especially when there were other people present.

She intercepted exchanged, meaningful looks and raised eyebrows, and knew that their parting was public knowledge and being gossiped about all over the hospital.

Somehow she managed to hold on to her calm smile, look impervious and unaware, but she hated knowing that people were talking about her; she hated knowing that David had been hurt and was angry with her.

There was just nothing she could do. If she could, she would have explained to him that she was a victim, too. She hadn't chosen to fall in love with someone else; it had hit her like a speeding truck and wrecked her life. She didn't try to explain, however. David had reacted as you would expect, like a surgeon, cut her out of his life at once and without compunction, and Luisa respected his decision.

She soon knew when David started dating someone else. Nobody told her directly, but remarks were dropped, rather obviously, when she was nearby, and one of the staff nurses on Women's Surgical, a petite blonde with a perfect skin and big blue eyes, began to go pink whenever she saw Luisa.

It didn't hurt, because Luisa had never been in love with David, but she couldn't help a little prickle of jealousy when she finally saw the two of them together, walking towards the hospital car park. They weren't holding hands, but almost—their hands kept brushing and Louisa felt a dart of memory. She and David had held hands on walks through the countryside, had smiled at each other like that. Before she met Zachary West and discovered the difference between the warm affection she felt for David and the fierce heat of desire she felt for Zachary.

Turning away, she scolded herself. What was the matter with her? She had no business being a dog in the manger about David. She wished him well; he was a nice man and deserved to be happy. The truth was, she envied him and his new girl their intimacy, the sense one had that they walked in a private world where only two could go.

The day before her father's court case was scheduled he rang to remind her in case she should want to attend.

'You won't be wanted to give evidence, though, so if you would rather not . . .'

She had offered to give evidence but his lawyer had said it wasn't necessary since they were not disputing the cause of the accident. Harry Gilbey was admitting the facts as put forward by the other side: that he had been over the central line as he came round the bend, driving very fast. His lawyer was hoping that he could claim that Zachary West, too, had not been giving full attention to the road ahead, or he would have seen the other car.

Luisa hadn't breathed a word to anyone about what Zachary had told her, about the girl he had seen walking in a garden. Frowning now, she wondered if she should mention it. Had his mind been elsewhere when he was faced with her father's car hurtling towards him? And did that absolve her father?

No, she thought. Zachary was on his own side of the road and driving quite slowly, she gathered. Whether he was thinking about a girl he had seen or not, the blame for the accident had to be laid entirely at her father's door.

And mine! she thought, guilt heavy on her heart. If I hadn't rung Dad . . . if I hadn't been so childish and sorry for myself . . .

'The good news,' said her father cheerfully, 'is that the deal with Noelle's client in Birmingham is going ahead. We haven't finally settled on a figure yet because he wants his accountants to study the books first, but he seems a fair man. Tough, but fair. I like him, and I think he'll stick to his bargain. So, whatever happens in court, I feel much better about the future, darling.'

'I'm glad, Dad,' she said, but she still felt guilty because of her own part in the sequence of events that had led up to the accident.

Luisa looked at her watch as she hung up. It was three o'clock; she wasn't due on the ward until seven forty-five.

She hurriedly finished washing up, put on some make-up, and within ten minutes was driving out of town in the direction of the sea. The weather had turned mild: there had been rain overnight, a light south-westerly was blowing off the sea, and she saw snowdrops under the trees in people's gardens. Spring didn't seem so far off this afternoon.

She parked outside Zachary's gate and he looked out of the studio window as she got out of her car.

She walked towards the house, very conscious of him watching her, the warm wind tossing her hair around her face and making her dark grey pleated skirt fly upwards so that she had to keep pushing it down.

Zachary slid back the wide french windows and gave her a sardonic smile. 'I can guess why you're here!'

'I don't think you can!' she retorted.

'Want to bet?'

'I don't believe in gambling,' she said coldly. 'I came to offer you a lift to court. I remembered that you aren't driving your car at the moment, and it would save you getting a taxi.'

'How thoughtful,' he drawled. 'Are you hoping I'll be so grateful that I'll let your father off the hook, somehow?'

'I'm not that optimistic!'

'Just as well, because I can't,' he said shortly, then added in the same curt tone, 'If I could, I would, Luisa, but in a courtroom you have to tell it exactly how it was, and your father was driving on my side of the road, coming round a bend at racing speed. That's the truth and I shall have to tell it.'

'I wouldn't want you to lie,' she said, as he stepped back to let her walk past him into the studio. 'And will you tell the court that your mind wasn't completely on the road, either?'

'What?' His black brows met and she turned away, her mouth dry with nerves, gazing instead at some sketches pinned up on the wall: pencil and charcoal drawings of trees and birds. They were stunning, but she couldn't appreciate them while she was tensely aware of him behind her.

'You were driving along in a daze, weren't you?' she said huskily, hearing his breathing on the back of her neck.

'What the hell are you talking about?' he snarled, and she began to tremble with nerves, but she wouldn't let him bully her into backing down. She was determined to say what she had come here to say.

'You were too busy dreaming about the girl you'd seen to be concentrating on the road.'

There was a little silence, then he said, 'I was driving slowly on my own side of the road. Your father was entirely to blame for the accident.'

'Not entirely,' she said with husky determination. 'Maybe mostly...I don't deny that, and neither does he—but if you'd been alert, if you'd been concentrating more, instead of daydreaming about a girl, you might have avoided him.'

'I must have been crazy, telling you about that,' Zachary broke out fiercely, grabbing her elbows and swinging her round to face him. Her lashes fluttered down to hide her eyes; she couldn't look at him. Oh, not because he frightened her—although he did, when he scowled like that, his brows heavy above his silvery eyes and his mouth a hard, straight line. No, she couldn't meet his eyes because she was afraid he would see the look in hers, would read the wild emotion filling her as he came so close, touched her. She had given him two reasons for her visit—to offer a lift, and to point out that he, too, had not been entirely concentrating as he drove towards the bend in the road. There was a third reason why she was here. She had had to see him. It seemed like a year since they last met; the time dragged whenever he wasn't there.

'But you did tell me,' she whispered. 'And I think it is relevant. Don't you think you should tell the court, instead of letting my father take all the blame?'

He shook her, bending towards her. 'That's why you've been coming here, isn't it? To get something out of me that you can use against me in court! And you always look as if butter wouldn't melt in your mouth—the perfect nurse, calm and gentle, like the madonna in some medieval painting, with your smooth skin and wide blue eyes...'

She was so startled that she looked up, and Zachary's hands slid up her arms and dragged her nearer to him, his angry face bent down to hers.

'I should have known better,' he ground out. 'I should have remembered that whatever you look like you're still a woman, and women are the most devious, two-faced, treacherous——'

'No, don't,' she broke out in distress, her mouth quivering. 'I'm not like that! Don't say such things about me, Zachary; you don't believe I'm like that, do you? You can't...'

His angry stare seemed to dive down into her dark blue eyes and she couldn't look away. Hypnotised, she stared back, her head swimming and her mind empty of everything but him.

Zachary, Zachary, her mind was saying, as she looked at him, absorbing him like blotting-paper drinking up water.

His stare moved slowly over her uplifted face, from her eyes to her trembling, parted mouth. She had no idea what he was thinking and by then she didn't care. She only knew that she wanted him to kiss her so much that it was like a physical pain deep inside her, a gnawing hunger that made tears start into her eyes.

Zachary saw them and frowned. 'Don't!' he muttered. 'Why do women always cry when they're losing an argument? It's one of their tricks for getting their own way.'

He put a hand up to her face, brushed his fingertips across her wet lashes, and looked at the trace of tears on his skin.

'And they're real, too,' he said disbelievingly.

'I hate you,' Luisa sobbed angrily, meaning it, hating him at that second almost as much as she loved him.

'Stop crying; you win,' he said with a wry groan. 'I'll admit in court that I wasn't concentrating completely when your father came round that bend. Anything to stop you crying. I can't stand it; you look so helpless and defeated.'

She smiled radiantly, like a rainbow, through tears which seemed to be flooding down now. 'Will you? Really? Oh, thank you...'

'Don't I get a reward for that?' Zachary softly asked, and slowly bent his head. She swayed towards him languorously, weak with desire.

At the first touch of his mouth her eyes closed, fierce pleasure stabbing her. She had been dying to kiss him ever since she walked into the room; the satisfaction of her need was almost unbearable.

Zachary slid her coat down over her arms, let it drop to the floor, his arms going round her. She yielded to them, her own hands clasping the back of his head, her fingers running through his thick black hair, feeling the powerful structure of the bones beneath it.

Zachary was breathing oddly, shifting restlessly as he kissed her, his hands moving, caressing, moulding her body with exploring, stroking fingers, as if he was learning the shape of her like a blind man discovering through his fingertips what he could not see.

Suddenly he broke off his kiss and buried his face in the side of her neck, his breathing hot against her skin.

'You baffle me,' he muttered. 'So cool on the outside, but all this passion underneath ... you're an iceberg, aren't you? Only a fraction of you shows above the surface, and I think you'd wreck anyone who was careless enough to collide with you.'

Hurt, she burst out, 'How can you say such cruel things? You don't know me...'

He lifted his head to look at her, his eyes impatient, wry. 'Do you think I don't realise that? I haven't an idea what goes on inside your head, and when I'm with you I never seem to understand what goes on inside my own head, either!' His mouth twisted cynically. 'For instance, why do I keep finding myself kissing you?'

She went dark red, biting her lip. 'Are you saying I throw myself at you?' Had he begun to guess how she felt about him? She could have sunk through the floor.

Zachary shook his head, his mouth crooked. 'No, of course not. You're much too classy, and if you were the type to chuck yourself at me I'd avoid you, believe me. That sort of woman makes me run a mile. No, I know the first move always comes from me.'

'Why ask me why you keep finding yourself kissing me, then? If you know you make the first move, you answer the question!' Luisa's voice was breathless; she wished she knew the answer herself.

Zachary let go of her and walked away, his hands in his pockets and his black head bent. 'I can't, and I wasn't asking you for answers, either—I was just thinking aloud, or trying to. I've been puzzling over the effect you have on me for days without coming up with any answers. Maybe something drastic happened to my brain in the crash, without it showing up on any of their X-rays.'

Luisa quickly reassured him. 'There's nothing wrong with your head. I've seen your X-rays and the brain scans. No brain damage at all.'

'I keep forgetting you're a nurse,' he wryly said. 'But that doesn't help. Maybe I spend too much time alone. I think too much and lately I keep finding myself thinking about you...'

She felt her heart turn over, then remembered the other girl, the one he had seen before the accident and dreamt about ever since.

'What about your girl in white, in the garden?' she murmured huskily. 'Don't you think about her any more?'

'All the time,' he said, that look of bewilderment on his face. 'I still dream about her, but sometimes....' He broke off, frowning.

'Sometimes what?'

Zachary didn't answer. He was standing in front of the easel in the centre of the room, staring at a canvas on it, his hands still jammed in the pockets of the blue jeans moulded to his lean body. She watched him, thinking how devastatingly sexy he looked, wearing just those jeans and a thin white sweater under which he wore nothing and which clung to his body like another skin.

She swallowed and walked over to join him.

'Are you painting yet?' she asked, turning to look at the canvas.

'I don't want anyone to see this!' he angrily broke out, moving to block her view, his broad shoulders crowding out the canvas, but too late. She had already seen the painting.

It wasn't finished, but the outlines were all there—trees, hedge, the dusky evening sky with a sickle moon drifting through it, and in the foreground a blur of white, a woman's figure in a floating white dress, with black hair hanging down around her shoulders and her face half turned away.

Luisa had known at once what she was looking at—a painting of the woman Zachary had seen in the garden that evening. It had all been there, the details he had described to her. Jealousy made her ultra-sensitive; she took it all in at a glance. The picture had a strangely magical quality: the half-light, the girl in her ethereal dress, the moon behind the trees' silvering leaves and the windows of a house glimpsed vaguely in the distance. It puzzled and intrigued, left you sure that there was some mystery behind the painting.

And then her eyes had flickered over the girl's averted face and widened in shock and disbelief. The face was her own.

CHAPTER NINE

While she worked that evening, Luisa kept remembering that moment. She had been so stunned that she hadn't even asked Zachary to explain; she had just turned and stared at him, her eyes wide.

He had gone dark red. 'I can't quite remember her face any more,' he had muttered offhandedly. 'I remember the impression it made on me, and when I'm dreaming about her I see her face clearly, but when I was doing the preliminary sketches for this I had to leave her face blank, and when I came back to it I still came up empty-handed every time I tried to draw it. I thought of leaving her face a blank—it would have been interesting, might even have made it a talking point. Clever stuff like that amuses the art crowd. But I'm not that sort of painter. I'm not into playing tricks and games to make an impression. Then while I was trying to decide what to do I found myself doodling eyes, nose, a mouth... and when I stepped back to look at it, it was you. And it looked right,' he had said with a shrug. 'So when I did the actual painting I put your face in.'

He had stared at the canvas, his mouth hard and wry, and Luisa had watched, wishing she knew what he was thinking.

Giving her a veiled look, he had asked, 'Do you mind?'

She had shaken her head, speechless. Mind? Her heart had been beating so fast that she felt sick. But what did it mean? Why had he painted her face in this picture of his dream girl?

His voice had roughened. 'Maybe now you see why I said I was confused about you... it isn't only you that's baffling me. I'm baffled myself. I keep finding you in my arms, and now when I try to paint her face I find I'm painting yours. It's as if two images have merged inside my head, but I don't understand why! What the hell has happened to my mind?'

Luisa hadn't got an answer to give him. Thinking about it that night while she moved around the ward, she contemplated talking to one of the hospital's psychiatrists. But they wouldn't give her a snap judgement, off the cuff; quite rightly they would call that unprofessional.

They would want to see Zachary, assess him over a long period, and she had a shrewd idea that Zachary wouldn't agree to see them. He had seen too many doctors over the past year, for one thing, and, for another, he had been pretty scathing about psychiatry when they touched on the subject. He had strong views about that, as he had about everything else.

She had arranged to drive out to the cottage next day to pick Zachary up and drive him to court.

'You're early,' Zachary said, opening the door to her, strangely formal and unlike himself in a dark suit and a striped red and white shirt with a maroon silk tie. Luisa preferred him in his old blue jeans and body-hugging white sweater.

'Well, there isn't much room in the court-house car park,' she explained. 'So I thought I'd drop you and then find somewhere to park.'

He gave her a hard stare. 'I see. And, of course, you aren't too keen on being seen walking into the court with me!'

She flushed and tried to change the subject. 'Don't forget your seatbelt, will you?'

Ignoring the reminder, he turned and looked at himself in her driving mirror, his mouth tightly reined. 'I realise people are going to stare when I walk in there. Maybe I should wear a bag over my head?'

His voice was so harsh that she winced as if he'd hit her. 'Don't talk like that. You have a few scars——'

'A few?' His mouth twisted; he gave his reflection another bitter glance.

'Some people may stare,' she softly said. 'But only at first; they'll soon get used to the way you look.'

He slowly turned his head to stare at her. 'You only say that because you're used to seeing people with bad burns.'

'No,' she firmly insisted, 'I say it because I've noticed over the years how patients and their families cope with facial disfigurement. The human mind is amazing; people get used to all sorts of injuries and disabilities. Scars become invisible after a while; people no longer notice them because they expect to see them. We all have a façade people recognise, and any scar becomes part of that. It's only strangers who stare.'

'Today I'll be walking into a room full of strangers!' Zachary bit out, and Luisa looked down at his hands. They were clenched into fists. She picked them up, first one, then another, and, finger by finger, unclenched each hand.

'Don't get so tensed up! If you don't know them, why should you be worried what they think? Walk into that courtroom with your head up and if people stare, let them.' She let go of both hands and moved back in her seat, her face pink and her eyes lowered. 'You ought to be used to being stared at, anyway. You're a very attractive man...'

His mouth twisted into a sneer. 'I saw how attractive I am now, when Dana looked sick as soon as she set eyes on me!'

'Oh, her!' Luisa crossly shrugged the memory of Dana away. She had never met her, but she knew she would not like her. 'Who cares what she thinks?'

He suddenly laughed. 'True. Who cares what Dana thinks?' He caught hold of Luisa's chin in one hand and pushed her head back so that he got a clear view of her face. 'Well, if you aren't ashamed of the way I look, why don't you want to be seen with me?'

She hesitated, her lashes flickering, her dark blue eyes restlessly meeting his then shifting away.

'The jealous boyfriend?' he curtly asked.

'Of course not!' she said, startled by mention of David when she rarely thought of him herself.

'He won't be there?' Zachary asked, and she shook her head blankly.

'Why should he be? He wasn't involved in the accident. It's nothing to do with him.'

'Are you still seeing him?'

Why was he so interested in David? 'We work together, so obviously I see him!'

Drily, Zachary said, 'You know what I meant. Are you dating him?'

'No, I'm not, as it happens!' she muttered, her lashes down against her flushed cheeks. 'Why are you asking all these questions about David?'

'I'm curious,' he coolly said. 'Is he still interested in you?'

'If you must know, he's dating a nurse from another ward!' She gave him a defiant look.

'Do you mind?' he persisted, holding her gaze.

She gave an irritated groan. 'You're like death or the tax man—you never give up, do you?'

'Not when I want an answer,' he said, looking amused. 'So tell me...do you mind knowing that he's dating someone else?'

'No, I don't,' she said with resignation. 'He wasn't important to me, and I wasn't the right woman for him, either. We liked each other, but no more than that. Now can we stop talking about my private life?'

'Not yet. Why was he so jealous that day he followed you to the cottage, if you weren't important to him?'

'David had fooled himself into believing I mattered to him, but he soon found himself another girl when he accepted that it was over.'

'Who ended it? You or him?'

'I did. I'd told him it was over before he followed me here that day. That was partly why he was so worked up...' She stopped dead, realising he might get the impression that her breakup with

David had something to do with himself, and hurriedly added, 'We had been arguing for weeks; it was nothing to do with you. It was just coincidence that he followed me here that day.'

'Hmm...' he said, sounding unconvinced. 'Did you ever think you loved him?'

The brusque question startled her. Wordlessly, she shook her head.

Zachary watched her intently. 'Have you ever thought you loved anyone?'

'Of course! What do you think? Years ago, when I was still in my teens, I fell in and out of love every other month.'

'And since then?'

She didn't answer that.

He smiled crookedly. 'That explains the way you look,' he murmured.

She was not going to ask him how she looked; she obstinately stayed silent, and after a moment Zachary asked, 'Then why are you afraid of being seen with me? Scared of people suspecting we were in collusion about the evidence?'

'No, of course not! But I... well, my father... I've never said anything about knowing you.'

He looked astonished, taken aback. 'Oh. I see. You haven't? So it wasn't his idea to...?' He broke off and she frowned, working out how he had been going to finish that sentence.

'His idea to what?' Then it dawned on her what he had meant and she angrily burst out, 'No! No, it wasn't my father's idea for me to drive you in! He doesn't know I've met you again, and I've never told him, or anyone, what you told me about the girl in the garden.'

There was a little silence, then he smiled at her. 'Well, shall we go? We've been sitting here for a good ten minutes arguing; we'll be late if we don't get a move on soon!'

He believed her. Relief flooded through her and she sighed, then she started the engine, backed into his drive, and swung the car round in the direction from which she had come. 'It shouldn't take more than half an hour to get to Whinbury. We won't be late, but it's lucky I left myself plenty of time.'

'You're always very cautious,' he drawled, amusement in his voice.

She knew he was teasing her, but she didn't rise to it. She was too worried about the outcome of the case, about her father's future. She seemed to have lost her sense of humour.

Zachary leaned back in the seat, watching the hedgerows flicker by, their bare black branches giving glimpses of ploughed fields and windswept pastures full of grazing sheep. 'There are snowdrops everywhere in my garden,' he told her. 'Only a couple of months and spring will be here. It was spring when the accident happened. A whole year ago. I've never known a year go so slowly.'

She stared ahead, feeling cold. He was still bitter and she couldn't blame him. He had had a bad time since the accident; his whole life had been turned upside-down.

'At least I'm painting again,' he said, his tone lifting. 'You've no idea how good that feels, to get back to work, to look forward to walking into my studio every morning and seeing what I did the day before hanging there waiting for me to go on with it.'

'I've never painted, but I can imagine how it must have felt not to be able to do the work you trained for and enjoy best,' she said huskily.

He shot her a look. 'Would you miss nursing if you had to give the job up?'

'Yes, badly. It's what I'm good at and there's a special thrill about doing something you know you can do well.'

'Yes, you're a good nurse,' he murmured. 'You know, it's odd—I do remember you vividly, although I was only in your ward for a short time. I have the clearest memories of you bending over my bed at night, looking like a cold angel, with your starched white cap and that calm oval face. I remember I resented you bitterly. I was in such pain and I was terrified I would die or be so horribly disfigured that I might as well be dead—and you seemed so cool and certain of yourself. I wanted to scream at you, yell my rage and resentment!'

'You did once or twice!'

He groaned. 'Did I really? Well, I apologise for that. Now that I know you I'm sure you were doing everything you could for me. It must have been a shock to get yelled at for it!'

'Don't be silly. We get used to it. People in pain can't be expected to behave like plaster saints.'

'You're very tolerant! But then you have a whole cluster of the virtues, don't you? You're gentle and compassionate, and calm and generous, and very forgiving. Stop!'

She jumped as he yelled the last word, completely at sea, turning bewildered eyes on him.

'Stop the car!' he ordered in a voice that scared her. She looked in the mirror, saw no car behind her, and there was no car coming towards them, so she put her foot on the brake and pulled into the kerb as the car rolled to a stop.

'What's wrong?' she asked, but Zachary didn't answer; he seemed to have forgotten her, in fact. He was opening the door; she watched him leap out of the car, turned in her seat and saw him dashing away, back along the road. Had he seen something on the road? She surely hadn't hit something?

Sometimes, driving along here in winter, a cock pheasant flew in front of the car, heavy and stupid with food, or a rabbit came out of the hedge and ran across the road, and one had to be very quick-witted to avoid hitting them. If there were other vehicles on the road it was often impossible to swerve out of their path or stamp on one's brakes, for fear of causing a serious accident, and then Luisa found it unbearable to have killed a living thing. Even worse if she injured but did not kill something that vanished into undergrowth before she could find it to take it to a vet. When that happened it could haunt her for days.

She had to know what she'd done. Reluctantly, she got out of the car and began to walk back towards where Zachary stood like a man turned to stone.

She looked around on the road, but could see nothing. 'What is it? What's wrong?' she asked Zachary, noticing his pale face with dismay, and he gave her a strange, dazed look.

'It was here!'

'What was? A bird?'

'A bird? No!' he ground out impatiently. 'That night...it was here...'

Luisa caught on at last. 'Where the accident happened? No, no, Zachary, you're wrong; that was much further on.' She knew the exact spot—she had driven over it many times in the past months, and each time she had felt her skin turn cold and her mouth go dry. He could so easily have been killed. So could her father.

'No, not the accident. Don't you understand? This is where I saw her.'

Luisa froze. 'Here? You saw her here?'

His eyes were fixed on the opposite side of the road where a hedge of hawthorn and elder ran, waist-high, tangled, leafless branches now, but last spring they had been rioting with new life and colour. There had been primroses under them, and violets and daffodils, and a few early bluebells creeping like blue mist under the trees.

'That hedge...I saw her floating along behind that hedge, in that garden. That house...do you see the white house set back behind the trees...? That must be her home.'

His voice wasn't quite steady; the words were faintly blurred. She could hear his breathing, see the misty coils of it on the winter air. He gave a husky laugh. 'She could be there now; she could come out, at any minute...'

Luisa was as white as a ghost. She stared through the wintry garden to the distant house as fixedly as Zachary did.

'You're sure this was the place?' she whispered, her ears singing with hypertension.

'Certain. I could never forget it. You saw my painting; don't you recognise it?'

'I didn't,' she said slowly. 'But then it never occurred to me... One garden looks much like another one, and the house wasn't very clear. I never suspected, not once.'

Zachary turned his head eagerly. 'You know this house? You know her? Who is she? What's her name?'

Luisa didn't answer. Her dark blue eyes lifted to him with a radiance in them, the sheen of tears and the glow of happiness.

For a long moment he just stared back at her, then his eyes widened and his face had the glazed incredulity of shock.

'It was my birthday,' Luisa said quietly. 'I always spent my birthdays with my father, but although he had promised to take me out he forgot and went off to a party with my stepmother. I drove over here to my old home, the house you see through the trees ... I lived there most of my life, until my father remarried. I thought Dad would be waiting for me. I'd bought a new dress, for my birthday. It was very romantic—filmy, white, with long sleeves and a lot of lace around the neck and hem. It had a faintly medieval look.'

'Yes,' Zachary said, his voice a mere thread of sound.

She waited, but he didn't say anything else so she went on, 'When I got here I discovered Dad wasn't in, of course. I was upset; I lost my temper. I got the telephone number of the place where the party was being held and I rang Dad and asked how he could forget my birthday. That was childish and stupid, and I wish to heaven I had had more self-control. I should have gone off to eat alone, or rung a friend—anything but act like a spoilt brat.'

He laughed shortly. 'You? Never in your life. A spoilt brat is something you've never been.'

She gave him a brief glance, smiling tremulously. 'You don't know me.'

'I'm going to,' he said, and her breathing almost stopped.

'I upset my father, though,' she went on in an unsteady whisper. 'He said he'd come at once; he told me to wait and he'd be there any minute. So I went out into the garden—it was a lovely spring night—and I walked down through the garden to meet him here.'

'You had your hair down,' Zachary whispered. 'Like a girl. It floated around your face as you walked, and your white dress drifted around you, too. You looked like a medieval virgin waiting for a unicorn, in a twilight garden. You were as calm and mysterious as moonlight.'

She laughed faintly. 'You're so romantic. You don't look it . . .'

'How do I look?' he asked, and his voice had grown bitter again. 'No, don't answer that—I know I look like something they scare kids with on Hallowe'en.'

'You don't! Your face is scarred and so is your mind, but you're still a very sexy man—but I'm sorry, Zachary, because it was my fault my father was driving too fast; it was my fault you've had all this pain.'

He looked searchingly into her face: the enormous dark blue eyes, the perfect skin, the tremulous lips. His gaze softened and he smiled at her.

'Maybe that was the price I had to pay to find you. Nothing comes for nothing.'

Her heart turned over.

'And I've learned a lot, about myself, and being alive, over this past year,' he said wryly. 'Maybe I'll be a better painter after this. I'll be a different sort of painter, anyway. I used to like painting landscapes—I never painted people if I could help it—and I realise now that I found people difficult to relate to; I preferred landscape because it didn't demand anything from me. But when I finally started to paint again it was a human figure I knew I needed to paint: the girl I'd dreamt about for so many nights, she . . . you . . . you were what I clung to all those months; you made me fight for my life.'

She was so moved that she couldn't speak. She remembered the first night he had spent in her ward, poised between life and death. She had kept walking down the ward to his bedside, staring at him lying there, utterly immobile in drugged sleep. It had never entered her head that he might be dreaming about her.

Zachary put an arm around her and led her across the road under the shadow of a laburnum tree which leaned across the hedge. He clasped her face in both hands, his gaze slowly wandering from her eyes to her nose and mouth, her neck, her swept-up hair.

'Promise me you'll always wear your hair down when you're not at work,' he said. He put a hand up and began to undo the pins that held her chignon in place. 'It takes years off you, don't you realise that?'

Huskily she laughed. 'Why do you think I wear it up? When I started on the wards the patients laughed at me and the doctors wouldn't trust me an inch because I looked like a little girl, so I started putting my hair up, so I'd look older.'

'Well, don't, any more,' he said, letting the heavy black strands fall through his fingers. 'It's like silk, black silk. I can't wait to see you naked with your hair falling down over your breasts...'

Her skin burned and she gasped.

He gave her a wicked, teasing look. 'I'm not going too fast for you, am I, my love? We've known each other almost a year; these days that's a long, long time.'

She was speechless, bright pink.

He smiled. 'You're blushing again—that should have given me an inkling long ago, the way you blush! It never did fit the image I had of Sister Gilbey, the iceberg in a starchy uniform. I could imagine the girl I'd seen in this garden blushing, though. I fell in love with her the minute I saw her walking in the twilight, but I ought to have remembered that the eyes can play tricks, especially at that hour. I thought I saw a young girl, and when I saw you again, in the ward, in your uniform, I didn't recognise you at all. You seemed so different, but my eyes were still playing tricks, weren't they? The tall, calm nurse who bent over my head like a cold angel in the night was the same as the girl I had been dreaming about. The difference was all in my mind.'

Her throat closed up and anxiety made her tense. 'Are you saying you imagined how you felt?'

'No, Luisa,' he said softly. 'It wasn't my feelings which were the problem; it was my mind. I read coldness in your manner; it was never there, was it? And I resented you because I associated you with my pain, when the truth was that you were trying to ease it. But at the same time I was always attracted to you, and that confused me because I was dreaming at night of one woman, and when I was awake I kept wanting to kiss another one. When the two of them began to merge I thought I was really in trouble. You can't be in love with two women at the same time, and you can't confuse one with the other without needing psychiatric help.'

'I thought you might,' she confessed, suddenly laughing as it dawned on her that all her anxiety about him had been a delusion, that she had been the two women he had been painting.

'I know, I saw your expression that day, when you looked at my painting and saw your own face on what was supposed to be another woman's body. I should have known then, too. I couldn't picture the face I'd seen any more; I could only see your face. That should have told me.'

'I hoped it meant you were turning to me and forgetting her,' Luisa said, and Zachary drew a sharp breath.

'Luisa ... darling ... I just told you I love you. How do you feel about me?'

'Don't you know?' she said, laughing and husky. 'I'm crazy about you. I have been in love with you ever since they brought you into my ward looking so helpless and ill.'

He gave her a rueful look. 'But will you go on loving me when I'm not helpless and ill any more?'

Then his mouth swooped down and they kissed hungrily, their arms around each other and their bodies clinging.

Zachary lifted his head, breathing hard. 'I feel light-headed. I'm not dreaming, am I, darling? This is real, and you're actually here?' He stroked her cheek with one hand and she smiled at him, her mouth quivering, and then suddenly caught sight of the watch on his wrist and gave a groan of dismay.

'Look at the time! We're going to be late for court!' She pulled away and began to run back towards the car and Zachary came after her.

As she started the engine again he reassured her, 'You've got three quarters of an hour to get me there; that's plenty of time.'

She just made it, dropping him off before going to find a parking place. Zachary lingered a moment before getting out of the car, insisting on a kiss.

'Go on! You mustn't be late!' she urged, pushing him away with one hand, but her mouth clung to his and he detached himself reluctantly.

Luisa had a problem finding somewhere to park. By the time she got back the case had started and she slid into a seat in the public benches, her anxious eyes moving from her father to Zachary and then on to the faces of the magistrates and the lawyers.

The winter sun shone down through the windows and carved cruel lines in her father's face, made him look older. The cold sunlight did Zachary no favours, either. It illuminated his scarred face ruthlessly: Luisa winced as she saw people in the court staring at him. He was gazing at the floor, his jaw clenched, and she knew he was conscious of being stared at. She saw the lividity of the scars, white against his healthy skin.

Her heart ached for him, for both these men, whom she loved. It was a bitter irony that they should have met that way, in a crash that had wrecked both their lives, and that they should be here, opposed, in a court of law, like duellists. She was afraid of the outcome of this case. Justice for Zachary could mean ruin for her father—and how could she then tell her father she loved the man who had wrecked his life?

The case dragged on slowly, relentlessly, hour after hour. The lawyers droned, the magistrates asked questions, her father and Zachary both gave evidence, and so did the police and ambulancemen who had first come on the scene after the accident.

Harry Gilbey looked stunned as Zachary, giving his evidence, confessed that he had been abstracted that night. 'I have to admit I had my mind on other things or I might have seen the car coming towards me and been able to swerve out of his way before he hit me,' he said, and Harry Gilbey gave him an incredulous, grateful look.

As the time ticked by Luisa found it harder and harder to stay awake in spite of her anxiety and distress. She had had no sleep today; she had been on night duty yesterday. Thank heavens she was not working tonight, but in the stuffy atmosphere of the court her head kept nodding forward during the dull police evidence.

The court's decision, when it finally came, was no surprise. Harry Gilbey was found to be largely responsible for the accident, which meant that damages would be awarded to Zachary West, both for his personal injury and for the loss of his paintings, but the amount would be determined at another date.

Everyone began to leave. Luisa stumbled out of court, heavy-eyed, a little confused.

Her father came out with Noelle and his solicitor, and she went over to give her father a kiss.

'How do you feel, Dad?'

'Glad it's all over,' he said, grimacing.

'But they didn't say how much the damages would be!'

'Apparently that's a specialised subject. Zachary West will have to submit an audited breakdown on the loss he suffered.'

'He'll probably double the figures he first thought of,' Noelle said furiously.

At that moment Zachary walked towards them, and Harry Gilbey gave him a shy, uncertain look, offering his hand.

'Mr West... I'm very sorry...and thank you for what you said in court; it was very honest and generous of you...'

Zachary shook hands, smiling at him. 'It was the truth, and, anyway, I had an ulterior motive for being honest.'

Harry Gilbey looked at him uneasily. 'Oh? What was that?'

Zachary slid his arm around Luisa's waist in a possessive gesture. 'I want to marry your daughter,' he said, and Harry Gilbey's jaw dropped.

He was not as astonished as Luisa, who nearly fainted. She lifted her dark blue eyes to him and

Zachary smiled down at her, passion and amusement in his face.

'Am I going too fast for you, again, my love?'

'Luisa?' her father asked, meaning, Luisa, you never told me, I had no idea you ever saw him again—what has been going on?

Noelle was too stunned to say anything but she was staring incredulously, her eyes going from Luisa to Zachary, and back again.

'No, you aren't going too fast,' Luisa said to Zachary, breathlessly laughing and throwing pride to the winds. 'I'd marry you tomorrow. Shouldn't we take time to talk it over first?'

'Cautious and practical as ever!' he said with apparent satisfaction. 'Yes, you're right. I just thought I should put your father in the picture and make it clear that my intentions were honourable.'

'Luisa,' her father pleaded, 'I don't understand. You've never said a word about... You've been seeing him? Why haven't you told me?'

'It's ... oh, can't you see ... it was difficult ...?' she stammered, and then Zachary intervened firmly.

'I think we should all go back to your house, Harry... may I call you Harry? Good. Well, let's go back to your house, and Luisa and I will tell you all about it. And, by the way, just forget about the damages—I certainly don't intend to start married life by screwing every last farthing out of my new father-in-law.'

Harry Gilbey stammered incredulously, 'B...but...are you...s...sure?'

'Of course he is,' Noelle quickly said, frowning impatiently at her husband. She turned a honeyed smile on Zachary. 'Very generous of you, Zachary, and very wise, now that you will be one of the family.'

'Thank you, Noelle,' he said gravely, but Luisa caught the glint of cynical amusement in his eyes. Noelle was beautiful, but she didn't fool Zachary the way she had Harry Gilbey.

The arm around her waist tightened and Luisa looked up at him, her black hair loose around her flushed face and her heart in her eyes, silently telling him how grateful she was to him for that gesture.

'Shall we be on our way?' he asked her. 'We have a lot to tell your father and stepmother, after all! It is going to take some explaining!'

She nodded, but couldn't help thinking that they would never be able to explain the whole story. They would tell them they were in love, but there was a lot they would leave out, many things too private to be talked about. How could you explain that Zachary had been in love with her before he knew it was she he was in love with? How could you explain that she had fallen in love with him when he was unconscious, his face just a mask? Who would ever understand? Luisa didn't understand it herself, and she knew Zachary didn't, but maybe one day he would paint pictures that would illuminate the mystery for both of them and then the whole world would see the way they loved each other.

POSTCARDS FROM EUROPE

HARLEQUIN
PRESENTS®

Hi—
It's carnival time in
Italy! The streets of
Venice are filled
with music—the
costumes are
incredible. And
I can't wait to
tell you about
Lucenzo Salviati...
Love, Meredith

*Travel across Europe in 1994 with
Harlequin Presents. Collect a new
Postcards From Europe title each month!*

Don't miss
MASK OF DECEPTION
by Sara Wood
Harlequin Presents #1628

*Available in February wherever
Harlequin Presents books are sold.*

HPPFE2

**Relive the romance...
Harlequin and Silhouette
are proud to present**

A program of collections of three complete novels by the most requested
authors with the most requested themes. Be sure to look for one volume each
month with three complete novels by top name authors.

In January: **WESTERN LOVING**   Susan Fox
                                             JoAnn Ross
                                             Barbara Kaye

Loving a cowboy is easy—taming him isn't!

In February: **LOVER, COME BACK!**   Diana Palmer
                                             Lisa Jackson
                                           Patricia Gardner Evans

It was over so long ago—yet now they're calling, "Lover, Come Back!"

In March: **TEMPERATURE RISING**   JoAnn Ross
                                             Tess Gerritsen
                                           Jacqueline Diamond

Falling in love—just what the doctor ordered!

Available at your favorite retail outlet.

REQ-G3

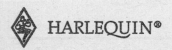 

Are you looking for more titles by

CHARLOTTE LAMB

Don't miss these fabulous stories by one of
Harlequin's great authors: